ABOUT THE BOOK

Have you ever thought what it might be like to live on your own for a while? Charley is a girl who not only thinks about it—she actually does it. Believing that no one wants her, Charley runs away and finds that being on her own can be both an exciting adventure and a very lonely experience. She is faced with the everyday practicalities of what to eat and where to live, yet still has lots of time for her special world of enchantment and imagination. A series of strange and amusing events bring Charley home at last, but only after she has made some very important discoveries about herself and other people.

Set against the background of a charming British countryside, this story is written with warmth and understanding and a compelling touch of fantasy.

THORNLEY

Old Man's cottage

Mrs Denning's

The Horseshoe.

Bartlett's

Summerhouse

Scarecrow

A Map of the
neighbourhood
where Charley
spent her
unusual holiday

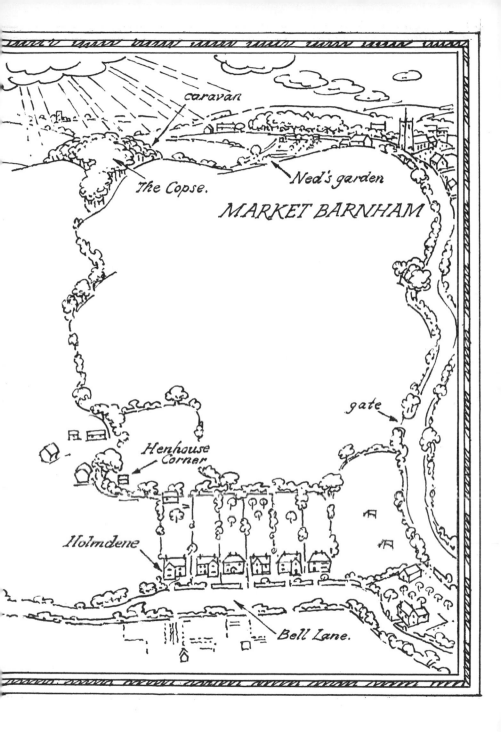

caravan

The Copse.

Ned's garden

MARKET BARNHAM

gate

Henhouse
Corner

Holmdene

Bell Lane.

CHARLEY

CHARLEY

Joan G. Robinson

Illustrated by
Prudence Seward

Coward-McCann, Inc.   New York

Contents

CHARLEY

1

Charley

"I'll run away," said Charley, "that's what I'll do."

She got off the bed, where she had been sprawling in muddy gum boots ever since the row with Aunt Emm, and rummaged in the cupboard for her case. It was small, barely more than doll's size, and made of cardboard, but it would do. She would not need much. Just the remains of the nut toffee bar and one or two other things, some paper to write on, perhaps a book to read.

"That'll show them," she said, shoving the things in, higgledy-piggledy, *"that'll* show them."

Another bar of nut toffee lay unopened on the chest of drawers. It was Toby's. *What if it is?* she thought. *Aunt Emm will buy him another as soon as he asks for it. She'll never have to buy me another. Serve her right. Serve them all right.*

She went quietly downstairs and out through the side door. "Serve them right," she said to herself again as she set off toward the common. "Aunt Emm won't be quite so sure she's a good manager when she hears I'm lost. I bet Mother and Dad will have something to say when they hear about it. Perhaps I'll never come back. *Then* she'll be sorry."

On the edge of the common she sat under a hawthorn bush and watched the children in the distance playing on the swings. The grass was dusty and dry and littered at intervals with ice-cream cartons. It looked tired already, although it was only July. Charley hated everything: the swings, the children, the litter, even the grass.

Angrily munching her way through both bars of toffee, she went over in her mind all that had gone wrong. It was Aunt Emm's fault. She should never have come. Last time Dad had gone abroad to work, and Mother had gone with him, Auntie Louie had come to look after them and that had been quite fun (Auntie Louie was not a real aunt, but had once been a neighbor). And the time before that it had been Granny. It had only been a few weeks then. Now they had gone for much longer, Granny was too old to cope with all three of them, and Auntie Louie had married someone called Mr. Hewitt who didn't like children. So Aunt Emm had come. Beastly old Great-Aunt Emm, who let Giles do what he liked (because he was the oldest), and always made a fuss over

14

Toby (because he was the youngest), but never, never let Charley do anything at all.

Her eyes smarted at the unfairness of it. She had almost looked forward to Aunt Emm coming in the beginning, feeling it might be a sort of second chance, a fresh start. She would be helpful, she had decided. She and Aunt Emm might do the baking together. Perhaps go shopping, share the secrets of present buying when Christmas came, make the puddings. The two of them—looking after the boys.

One of the angry tears overflowed—a hateful feeling—and trickled sluggishly down her cheek. Charley made a face, partly to stop more tears overflowing and partly to show herself what she thought of herself. Silly fool that she was, ever to have thought it could be like that. When she had tried to help Aunt Emm by telling her how her mother did things, Aunt Emm had told her not to interfere. When she did nothing, Aunt Emm had called her lazy. Whatever she did was wrong.

The children were squealing on the distant swings, jostling each other for turns. Their voices echoed across the common like the cries of angry sea gulls. Charley watched the usual ritual without interest, her mind still on Aunt Emm.

Today the row had been over a silly little thing— the garden hose. She had been showing Toby how to make the water go farther by covering half the nozzle with her fingers, when suddenly a stream of water

15

had shot out sideways and through the window. She had quickly turned the hose away, soaking Toby with the full jet of water by mistake. Dropping the hose, she had run, dragging him behind her. In the tool shed she had wiped him down with a handkerchief, made him promise not to tell, and suggested they go back into the house by different ways. But Aunt Emm had been sitting near the window, writing letters, and had caught the stream of water herself, so there had been a row as soon as Charley appeared again.

Well, perhaps that *had* been Charley's fault (by mistake), but it was not only Charley who had spoiled everything. It had been spoiled for her before it had ever begun.

Aunt Emm had come over to see them before their parents went away—none of the children remembered ever having met her before—to talk to their mother about all the things she would need to know: shops, laundry, early closing days, things like that. Giles and Toby had been in the garden, and Charley had been painting at the dining-room table while her mother and Aunt Emm sat talking in the sitting room.

Charley had not listened to what they were talking about until she heard her mother say, "I don't think you'll have much trouble with the children." Then she had pricked up her ears.

"Of course Toby's chest is a little weak," her moth-

er had said, "he'll need keeping an eye on occasionally. Giles is as tough as nails, thank goodness. As for
Charley . . ." Her voice had dropped then; there had
been a pause, then the sound of a door closing.

Immediately Charley had felt uneasy. "As for me—
what?" she had asked herself, and got up quietly and
gone out into the hall to listen. But she had only been
able to hear the murmur of her mother's voice behind the closed door.

What had her mother been saying to Aunt Emm?
What might she have been saying? That Charley was
greedy? That she was bad-tempered? That she bul-
lied Toby sometimes? Perhaps she was warning her
that she might be difficult on occasions, refusing to
go to sleep when the others did, then finding any
excuse to go downstairs for a minute, asking for a
drink of water, pretending she had forgotten the
book she would want to read in the morning, saying
she was sure Toby was coughing when she knew very
well he was sound asleep—making up any old story,
in fact, in the hope that she might be allowed to stay
downstairs a little longer.

As her mother always pointed out, it was unfair.
Worse than that, it was dishonest. It was a lie to say
Toby was coughing when he wasn't, just because she
wanted to stay up a little later than the others. That
was cheating. Was her mother telling Aunt Emm now
that Charley was deceitful, that she told lies?

Scowling, she had mixed a pool of black paint in

the palette and put a large black cloud at the top of her picture. No, probably her mother had just been warning Aunt Emm. Warning her not to be too lenient, telling her how to cope with Charley. To be kind but firm, to be busy and brisk and matter-of-fact . . .

It was a pity that Charley had overheard those few words. It meant that when Aunt Emm and Mrs. Weston came out of the sitting room ten minutes later, she was already on the defensive.

"Ah, here's Rowan," said Aunt Emm. "Or am I to call her Charley, too?"

"Oh, yes, do! I doubt if she'd answer to Rowan now, she's been Charley for so long!"

It was true. She had been called Charley almost as long as she could remember. It had started one day, long ago, when she had been dressed up in an old evening gown of her mother's, and the paper boy coming up the path to the house, had seen her standing inside the window, flapping imaginary wings. As she had also been wearing a wastepaper basket on her head—being still young enough to imagine that if she could not see, neither could she be seen—she must have been a rather remarkable sight. The paper boy had evidently thought so, and had turned to Giles who was playing in the garden, saying, "My! She looks a proper charley, don't she!" Giles had been delighted with this remark, and although Mother had forbidden him to keep on repeating it, the name had stuck. Now she was called Charley by everybody.

"Well, Charley," said Aunt Emm, peering over her shoulder at the half-finished painting, "that's a nice picture. What is it, exactly? A little brown dog, is it—lost in a wood?" Charley did not reply. "And what's this big black cloud?"—Aunt Emm was really trying—"Is it a storm coming on?"

"I've just put that in," Charley mumbled.

"Oh. Poor little dog!" said Aunt Emm brightly.

"It isn't a dog," said Charley.

Aunt Emm abandoned the painting and looked at Charley. "Well, dear, I hope we shall get on together while Mother's away," she said in a brisk, firm voice. "Do you think we shall?"

Charley mumbled something.

"Speak up, my love," said her mother, in what the children called her "visitors' voice."

"Not particularly," said Charley.

Mother looked embarrassed and Aunt Emm laughed. "Don't worry, my dear," she said. "I'm sure we shall manage perfectly." She had looked at Charley then with a thoughtful, brooding expression and added, "Children aren't usually difficult with me for long. There are only one or two things I will *not* tolerate."

To Charley it had sounded like a threat.

2

About Lizzie Scrotton

The sun had gone in and the sky was clouding over.

Charley realized suddenly that the children had left the swings and that at any minute it was going to pour with rain. She got up, stretched herself and shivered. She should have brought a duffel coat if she was going to stay out all night. Perhaps she would sneak back home now and fetch one.

On the way back the rain began to fall and she decided it was not worth worrying about the duffel coat. It would be better to hide in the tool shed until she was sure she had stayed away long enough to give Aunt Emm a proper fright. That should be good enough. She stayed crouched in the tool shed, listening to the rain drumming on the roof, until she was cramped with cold. Then she crept stiffly around to the garden door and tiptoed into the house.

Everything seemed as usual. Upstairs she could hear Aunt Emm talking to Giles about what clothes he would be taking away with him when he went to stay with his friend, Peter Barrett, during the holidays: "Two underpants, two pajamas, you won't need your football jersey . . ." Anyone could tell just from the sound of her voice that Aunt Emm had once been a matron in a boys' school. From the kitchen came the sound of Mrs. Scrotton, the daily help, singing tunelessly to her transistor. Was it possible Charley had not been missed after all?

Quietly she opened the door of the rumpus room. Toby was sitting huddled close to the fender with his head in his hands. He looked up as the door opened.

"You took my toffee bar!" he said accusingly.

Charley glanced around quickly. "Did you tell?"

Toby shook his head. "Not yet. But I—"

"Come here." Charley took him by the arm and hustled him quietly upstairs. "Look, you can have this." She opened a drawer and brought out a red leather diary, the most cherished of her Christmas presents. "You always wanted that, didn't you? I've hardly used it."

Toby seized it; then his face fell. "You've wrote in it."

"It doesn't matter. Now shut up about it."

21

"But I want my toffee bar."

"I told you, you can have that instead." Toby's chin quivered. "All right, if you don't want it, I'll have it back." She made a lunge toward him, but he hugged it tightly to his stomach, both hands clasped in front of it.

"But I still want my toffee bar," he said plaintively.

Charley made another lunge. Toby shifted the position of the diary and Charley stopped, and stared. "What's that? Is it blood?" There was a bright-red stain on the front of his jersey.

"No, I—I think it's this." He held the diary up in the air, looking down at himself. "It's come off on it."

Charley caught hold of him. "But your jersey's sopping wet! Didn't you change it? Do you mean you've been going round in that ever since?" Toby nodded. "You silly little idiot! Why ever didn't you change it?"

"You told me not to tell."

"Well?"

"She'd have known if she'd seen me in another one." Toby's chin quivered again.

"Haven't you been cold?" He nodded and began to whimper. "And are you cold now?" He nodded again, and Charley saw that his teeth were chattering. She thought quickly. She must do something before he started crying properly.

"Oh, Toby, I'm sorry! No, don't cry. I'll tell you

what we'll do. I'm cold too. We'll do some exercises to warm us up, like proper athletes do." She pulled off his jersey and began rubbing his arms. They felt like thin cold sausages. "Now, jump up and down. Like this. I'll jump with you."

They took off their shoes and jumped and did every kind of physical jerk that Charley could think of; then Toby began coughing. They sat down on the floor and she put her arms tightly round him.

"I'll hug you warm. Poor Toby—poor little Toby. There—" She hugged him, rocking him to and fro and crooning softly. But Toby, grateful for the rare gentleness, was now melting into helpless tears. "*Now* what's the matter? Don't you like it?"

He nodded, gulped, then croaked, "S'nice. I like you, Charley."

"Stop crying, then, there's a good boy." She went on rocking him until her arms ached, expecting him to leap up at any minute, fully recovered, but he had relaxed and seemed to be dropping off to sleep. She looked at him in sudden alarm. "Oh, Toby, you're not going to be ill, are you? Please don't if you can help it!"

"I'll try not."

But Toby was going to be ill. Half an hour later there was no doubt about it. Aunt Emm had come into the rumpus room, where Charley was reading to him, taken one look at him (seeming not to notice

Charley at all), and hurried him upstairs to have his temperature taken. Then he was put to bed.

Charley went slowly along to the dining room, where Giles was working on his model plane.

"Toby's got a temperature," she said.

"I know."

"I think he's got a cold."

There was no reply to this. Charley stood watching for a moment, then asked casually, "What was for tea today?"

Giles glanced up. "What a silly question. You were here, weren't you?"

"You know I wasn't."

"Oh, no, perhaps you weren't. I'd forgotten."

"Did she notice?"

"Who—Aunt Emm? I shouldn't think so. Why should she?" He bent over the plane, holding a thin sliver of wood covered in glue. Charley watched as he lowered it carefully into place. Then he straightened his back and looked at her. "What are you waiting for? For me to say I missed you?"

"Don't be *silly*."

"Well, I noticed you weren't there, if that's what you want to know. And we had bread and cheese spread as usual, and one of Mrs. Scrotton's dough cake things." He bent over the plane again, adding casually, "If you really want people to think you've run away, you'll have to stay out longer than that.

Aunt Emm just thought you'd gone over to the common."

"But it was pouring!"

"Oh, yes—later. I told her then that you were probably in the tool shed. She said she thought you must be dotty. I tell you, if *I* had any such stupid idea as running away, I'd do it properly and make a job of it."

Charley turned away, looking scornful, as if such an idea had never occurred to her. But she was furious. Furious with Aunt Emm for not noticing, and furious with Giles for noticing and not caring. Furious with herself, too, for being the cause of Toby's cold. She had never meant that to happen.

She went along to the kitchen. Mrs. Scrotton, at any rate, would be glad of her company. Even if she was not, she would let Charley stay and talk to her. She might even be persuaded to tell her the story of Lizzie Scrotton again.

But Mrs. Scrotton had taken off her apron and was already pinning on her beret in front of the kitchen mirror.

"Oh—are you going?"

"Yes, just off. What was you wanting, love?"

"Nothing—nothing special."

Mrs. Scrotton, seeing the disappointment in Charley's face, sat down on a hard chair. "Well, stay and talk to me a jiff while I get me boots on. How's young Tobe? I heard him barking—a cold I shouldn't wonder."

Charley nodded. "Tell me about Lizzie, Mrs. Scrotton."

"Tell you about Lizzie?" Mrs. Scrotton threw up her eyes. "Well, you *are* a one for wanting the same story over and over! And what do you want me to tell about her this time? There ain't nothing more but what I've told you already."

"Didn't she really know where she was going to sleep at nights? Wasn't it queer, just walking from place to place and not living anywhere properly? Tell me about the lights in the houses, when it was getting dark in wintertime—"

The story of Lizzie Scrotton was a story of the bad old days, when poor people starved, and people without homes went tramping from workhouse to workhouse. Young Lizzie had never known anything else, Mrs. Scrotton said, until she'd come limping with her mother and little brother (and him a babe in arms) into Norwich one winter afternoon many years ago. There her mother had found a place, doing housework for an elderly clergyman who'd taken pity on them. But young Lizzie hadn't taken to it at first and she'd gone off on her own again. For the better part of a week she'd done the roads on her own, till the police had caught up with her at last. After that they'd all settled down and lived respect-

About Lizzie Scrotton

able. The exciting part of the story was that Mrs. Scrotton's husband had been none other than the babe in arms. "And-a-finer-man-never-broke-bread-may-he-rest-in-peace," she always added at this point, for Mrs. Scrotton had been a widow for many years.

His sister, Lizzie, had married a man who kept a poultry farm outside Royston, and now had children and grandchildren of her own, but often and often, when Scrotton were a little lad, she'd told him about when they was on the roads, and it only went to show—Mrs. Scrotton always ended the story like this— it only went to show, some people had a lot to be thankful for, what they didn't always realize.

But to Charley, the exciting part of the story was earlier, when Lizzie, trudging along the roads at twilight, would see the lights go on in the cottages, and, glancing in as she passed, see sometimes an old woman sitting in front of a blazing fire, sometimes children sitting up to tea around a table with a cloth on it.

"Tell me again how it looked to Lizzie when the lights went on," she said now, squatting beside Mrs. Scrotton as she struggled with the zip fasteners on her boots.

"Well, it's like I said"—Mrs. Scrotton fumbled for words—"to Lizzie—she always said it seemed as if those houses was the lights turned on in her own

27

home, because to her it seemed like the road *was* home, see? More than any houses was. So she didn't envy them, only thought it looked pretty and cozylike. After all, the only houses she'd ever been in was the workhouses, and nobody'd ever've called *them* cozy."

She got stiffly to her feet, put her slippers in her bag, and took her umbrella from the corner. "And now I must be off. But"—she paused with her hand on the latch, looking suddenly stern—"don't you never go thinking young Lizzie was lucky, because she wasn't. Not in them days she wasn't. You can think yourself lucky you're never likely to be in *her* shoes, and *that* I'm telling you!"

3

The Prize That Was a Surprise

Toby was ill for a week, and getting better for a week, and for a week after that he sat limply about the house, looking not very interested in anything.

By that time the school term was ending, Giles had fixed the date for his visit to Peter Barrett, and Aunt Emm, looking anxiously at Toby, kept saying what a pity it was that there wasn't a seaside holiday planned for all of them this year. She had a friend who ran a boardinghouse in Southsea, and might have written to her, only this would be her busiest time of the year.

On the last day of term Charley came home from school with a new paint box, wrapped in tissue paper in an oblong cardboard box. She left it casually on the dining-room table without a word, because she could think of no other way of breaking the astonishing news that she had won a prize—Miss Watson's prize for the Best Imaginative Painting.

She had been amazed, delighted, and appalled all at the same time. So utterly dumbfounded, in fact, that she had tripped over the step on her way up to the platform and lunged forward with both arms outstretched, coming to a stop in front of the lady mayoress only just in time. There had been a moment's stunned silence. Charley had muttered, "Suffering codfish!" under her breath, and the lady mayoress had smiled and said, "No hurry, dear." She had then given Charley her prize, and looked obviously relieved at the burst of applause and roar of laughter that had followed, growing louder every moment. Clearly the clumsy child was not unpopular. She did not know that Charley, walking sedately back to her seat, had been staring straight ahead of her with both cheeks puffed out to their fullest extent, and her eyes most horrifically crossed.

But, secretly, Charley had been appalled because, in a way, she felt as if she had been caught out cheating. Her painting had been pure accident, and that seemed much the same thing. Some of the others had tried hard, and worked on theirs. Hers had just happened. She had done it because she felt like it, not even remembering about the prize. And she knew she could never do it again.

All the afternoon she had felt uneasy about it. Later, Miss Watson had announced the usual holiday task. It was not compulsory, she reminded them, but it would be nice if everyone produced something, and this year it could be a subject entirely of their own choice, outdoor sketches, compositions, drawings, it did not matter what. "And we shall expect something from you this year," she had added, with an encouraging smile at Charley, "something really good." Charley had been even more dismayed. Miss Watson would have to go on expecting, she thought.

But the paint box was the one thing she had most wanted! She gloated over it secretly, wrapping and unwrapping it, and finally—still feeling almost as if she had stolen it—leaving it on the table until someone should notice it.

Giles saw it first. "Whose is this?" he asked.

"Mine," said Charley. "I got it for painting."

"What painting?"

"Oh—something I did," said Charley, mumbling because Aunt Emm was in the room.

"Oh, Charley, did you get a prize?" asked Toby, suddenly waking up to the situation. "Show me, what did you get?"

waiting for. "How *dare* you! You can go away at once. Language like that I will *not* tolerate!"

"Why not! It's English. His hand *is* bloody. Look at it."

Giles, tantalizingly, held his hand behind his back.

"Show me, Giles," said Aunt Emm. Giles showed her. There was a streak of blood, now dried, where he had cut it earlier with his penknife.

"You see?" Charley insisted. "It *is* bloody. I told him to take his *bloody hand off*, and that's what I meant." But she was only shouting for her own satisfaction. Aunt Emm had already taken Giles away to have a dressing put on it.

After that, to her relief, the subject of Charley's prize was dropped. In Aunt Emm's mind it had become associated with bad language. In any case, it would never do to encourage the child to be conceited, she thought, still worrying about how to get Toby to the seaside. Charley was difficult enough as it was.

The problem of how to get Toby away was happily solved only a few days later. Aunt Emm must have written to her friend after all, because a letter came inviting her and Toby to stay for a fortnight. It wouldn't be until September, her friend said, because the boardinghouse was full, but it was often better weather then and the sea air should set the little boy on his feet again.

Giles would be at the Barretts' at the same time, which was lucky. As for Charley, Aunt Emm was going to write to Mrs. Hewitt at Market Barnham to ask if she could have her there for a couple of weeks. Aunt Emm avoided Charley's eye as she said this, as if she were afraid Charley might think she was just being got out of the way, but Charley was delighted. Who wouldn't rather go and stay with Auntie Louie (even if her husband didn't like children), than go to a stuffy boardinghouse in Southsea with Aunt Emm?

The next few weeks flew by. Charley, who was to be the first to leave after all, could afford to be kind to the others, hoping they were not envying her too much for being the lucky one this time, and constantly reminding them that they, too, would be away by the end of the week. Aunt Emm was to see her off from the coach station, and she was to travel to Market Barnham by herself. Auntie Louie might not be able to meet the coach because she was working part time now—Aunt Emm was still waiting for confirmation on this—but in any case the stop was only a few minutes' walk from the Hewitts' house and Charley knew her way there.

She said good-bye to the others in high spirits. They stood around in the hall, waiting to see her off, while Aunt Emm gave last-minute instructions to Mrs. Scrotton about lunch and what to order from the baker. Then Aunt Emm came bustling out of the kitchen, made straight for the front door, and, with only the briefest "Hurry up, now" to Charley, set off down the garden path.

Charley seized her case, pulled her beret forward to exactly the same angle as Aunt Emm's, and followed, shoulders hunched, mouth pursed up disapprovingly, and feet turned out in such perfect imitation of her aunt that the others exploded into laughter behind her. Aunt Emm looked around with a startled face, and Charley did the same.

"What are they laughing at?" said Aunt Emm. "Is something wrong?"

"No, I think it was me," said Charley.

Aunt Emm looked at her quickly. "Well, if you *must* wear your hat at that absurd angle, it's enough to make anyone laugh," she said sourly, and flicked it back into place.

Charley agreed and danced happily along beside her. She would try and be nice to Aunt Emm now, just till they reached the bus station. Nothing, she thought, could spoil this wonderful, sunny, longed-for morning. She was going to Auntie Louie's, and soon she would be leaving Aunt Emm far, far behind.

It was only when she was in the coach and actually on the way to Auntie Louie's that she found the piece of paper that altered everything.

4

The Piece of Paper
That Altered Everything

Charley was already in her seat when Aunt Emm said, "Look, you'd better take this with you. It's got the address on it," and she had torn a strip off the top of a letter from Auntie Louie and slipped it to Charley over the top of the window. "Don't argue, now. I know you know where you're going, but it's better to have the address, all the same. I meant to put a label on your case, but there weren't any in the bureau, and I only bought some new ones this morning."

Aunt Emm had produced a new packet of labels and pushed one through the window. "You can write it now. Have you got your pen?"

The driver had climbed into his seat just then,

there had only been time for hurried nods and smiles, and Charley's last sight of Aunt Emm had been her waving the packet of labels and pointing to the one in Charley's hand, her whole face urgently reminding her not to forget.

Charley had not forgotten. She had searched around for the slip of paper, which had fluttered to the floor, and retrieved it from under the seat. And this is what she had found. Auntie Louie's address on one side,

Holmdene,
Bell Lane,
Market Barnham,
Norfolk,

and on the other side, in writing so large and legible that there could be no possibility of her being mistaken,

I don't want Charley. You know that. It's the work. Really I've got my hands full already. If it could . . .

That was all. The paper had been torn off before the next line. But it was enough. Enough to make Charley realize that she ought never to be on this coach at all.

She turned quickly, thinking for an instant that she might still be able to see Aunt Emm, to signal frantically that there had been a mistake, that she must get off the coach at once and go home again. Auntie Louie had written that she did not want her, and Auntie Louie never said things she did not mean. Charley could not possibly go and stay there now.

But in the next instant she realized that it was not only too late, *Aunt Emm must have known.* She had had that letter for a week or more. She had known Auntie Louie did not want her, but she had sent her all the same. It was a shock to Charley to realize how anxious Aunt Emm must have been to get rid of her. And it was a worse shock to discover that Auntie Louie had never wanted her at all.

She hunched her shoulders almost to her ears, jutted out her chin and stared doggedly at the road as it went flashing past. So Auntie Louie didn't want her. . . . Well, she didn't want Auntie Louie. Aunt Emm didn't want her either. She could certainly do without Aunt Emm. She could do without any of them. . . . She thought of Lizzie Scrotton. She had managed without anyone—until the police found her. But what was Charley to do now? Her fare to Market Barnham was paid. It was too late to go back.

"But I won't go," she said to herself. "*I won't go.* I'll run away instead."

But where could she run to? She had some money,

anyway, ten shillings pocket money and a pound in case of emergency. That would not take her far. But her clothes and things were packed and that was something. . . .

She gritted her teeth, and gradually, as the coach bounded along, a plan began to take shape in her mind.

At Market Barnham Charley got off at the stop before the usual one. Auntie Louie was not going to meet the coach but it was just as well to make sure. She walked along the grass, feeling that if she made no sound, she might somehow be less visible, but no one was about. It was the lunch hour. Even the cottages seemed asleep. About two hundred yards before coming to the marketplace she turned up the short road that led into Bell Lane, where Auntie Louie lived.

She must just go and have a look at the house— from a safe distance, of course. It seemed necessary to make sure it was still there. Holmdene was to be her center, she had decided. Not for anything would she actually go there, but she would skirt around it, always keeping it—for safety's sake—within reasonable distance. And she must be very careful not to be seen. The Hewitts must never know she had ever arrived in Market Barnham.

As she turned into Bell Lane, a tall gray-haired man appeared, walking down the road toward her.

She stopped dead. It was too late to run back. She went on again, walking now with a convincing limp. If you had one leg shorter than the other you could hardly expect to carry a heavy suitcase uphill without stopping occasionally. But you did *not* want to be helped. She tried swinging the suitcase casually as if it were only half the weight it was. It was hard work.

As they passed each other, the man smiled and said, "Good afternoon." She saw his collar and supposed he was the vicar. After a few steps she looked back and saw that he, too, had turned and was looking after her. She tossed her head, as a sign of her independence, and her beret fell off. She grabbed it and clapped it back on her head—flat like a pancake—praying it would stay balanced until she was out of sight, and limped on. The swinging suitcase knocked against her shins at every step, but she resisted the temptation to turn around again.

Probably he was wondering which house she was going to. Well, there were five or six to choose from. The Hewitts' was the last in a row of council houses, after which the land turned into a rough cart track that went on over the hill and wandered down into the next village.

She wondered whether the Hewitts went to church, and hoped not.

She went on until she could just see the chimneys of Holmdene rising over the other houses; then she stopped. It was unbelievably quiet. The only sounds were of a distant cock crowing and the faint humming of the telegraph wires.

Having satisfied herself that the house was still there, Charley turned back, went a short way down, then scrambled quickly through the hedge onto the lots on the other side of the lane from Holmdene. On the inside of the hedge she ran uphill again, until the rich brown earth, which looked like slabs of dark chocolate, clogged her shoes and made it impossible to run anymore. She struggled on, her suitcase seeming to grow heavier at every step, and her legs beginning to feel like lead, until she was well past the end of the houses. Then she crossed the cart track and went through into the opposite field. Now she was on the same side as Auntie Louie, but higher up.

She skirted the back of the house at a wide distance, dodging between haystacks and outhouses, until she reached a place she remembered. It was a meadow with a large chestnut tree in one corner, and the remains of what had once been a henhouse standing close beside it. The corner was bounded by an old wooden fence on one side, and on the other by a hedge that ran along the end of Auntie Louie's garden, and beyond.

Charley had played here only last summer when she had come to stay with Auntie Louie for a week while Mr. Hewitt was away. She had made the henhouse corner her secret place. It had the advantage of being only a little way from the end of Auntie Louie's garden, but—as the garden was long and narrow—well out of sight and earshot of the house.

Panting with heat, and exhaustion, and excitement, she dropped her suitcase and basket and sank down beside them into the long, cool grass.

Last summer this place had been her secret hideaway. Now it was to be her home.

5

A Drink of Water

The first thing Charley did was to take off her shoes and socks. Then she set about rearranging her suitcase. She rolled up her beret inside her blazer and put them to one end of the case, along with her white socks, and her best green dress—which she hated and Aunt Emm had insisted that she bring. She would not now need any of these. At the other end she put jersey, jeans, and all the other things she might be needing.

Her drawing things, and her new paint box still in its wrappings, went on a shelf in the hen house. She had not yet used the paint box, feeling it would be unbearable to be watched by Aunt Emm who, like Miss Watson, would now be expecting her to produce "something really good." (Silly creatures, both, to have thought her fawn was a dog!) Then she threw her shoes, heavy with caked mud, into the bottom of the hen house.

The next thing was lunch. Luckily she had brought this with her. She unpacked the basket with interest. There were two cooked sausages, a hard-boiled egg, and some bread and butter done up in greaseproof paper. Also two apples and a small packet of nuts and raisins. She decided to eat the sausages and some of the bread and butter now, and save the rest for supper. The apples would do for pudding, and the nuts and raisins for a snack in-between times.

The other things in the basket were a fruitcake for Auntie Louie from Aunt Emm, and a box of chocolates which Charley had been going to give her herself, because she was to have been the guest. She had paid for the chocolates out of her own money, so she could eat those herself. She had never owned a whole box of chocolates before and hoped she was not going to eat them all at once. Afraid that she might, she decided to ration them out to herself, two at a time, the way they always did at home.

A small greasy-looking packet in brown paper turned out to be a dough cake which Mrs. Scrotton must have slipped in at the last moment. That was nice of her, Charley thought, and it was going to be very useful now.

She ate her sausages and bread and butter, lying in the grass and listening to the gnats droning in the hedge, and the far-off bleating of a goat. It all seemed so familiar it was hard to realize that this was real and not a game. She remembered that last summer she had left a jam jar in which she used to keep sweets, in the bottom of the hen house. She got up and went to look. It was still there, lying on its side.

It was empty. But it was like meeting an old friend. Even the label was still stuck to its side with the word "refreshments" on it in her own writing. She was surprised to see how badly she used to write, then remembered that that had been a whole year ago.

She threw her apple core into the hedge, realizing she was still thirsty. Water was going to be her next worry. She knew there was a garden tap at the back of Holmdene, but that was perilously near the house. She would have to get her water from somewhere else. For the moment she had the empty bottle which had held lemonade for the journey. That would hold enough for tonight at any rate. Tomorrow she must get something bigger. She stowed everything else away inside the hen house and, taking the empty bottle, set off in search of water.

She went the way she had come, up to the field and out on to the cart track. It would be safer than going down into Market Barnham. Auntie Louie might even now be on her way back from work and it would be awful to meet her coming up the lane!

It was a long walk. The track was bordered by low, straggly hedges, through which she could see over the fields, some rough with stubble, others already plowed. She saw no one all the way, except a solitary scarecrow standing stiffly in a field, wearing the remains of an old felt hat tipped forward over its head. "Hallo, Aunt Emm," said Charley, "your hat's crooked. That I will *not* tolerate."

Overhead the sun blazed. The sky was enormous and bright blue. There was no shade anywhere. Birds flew up suddenly out of the hedge as she passed, squawking in alarm; otherwise the only sound was the rattle of a distant stacking machine. She could have enjoyed the walk if only she had not been so thirsty. As it was, she grew hotter and drier every minute, and the cart track seemed endless.

The first house she came to was set back from the road in a large garden with a lawn and tidy flower beds. The geraniums looked even hotter than Charley felt, violently red, and smelling faintly of petrol. It was not the sort of house where you could ask for a drink of water.

She went on down, past a barn and some outbuildings, and came to a very small cottage, hardly more than a lean-to, and here she stopped. There was a triangular patch of garden in front of the cottage, a garden unlike any she had ever seen before. Instead of flowers, it was filled with brightly colored wooden toys. In the center of the grass stood a windmill painted blue and white, its tiny sails turning slowly. Below it a group of gnomes with pointed red caps appeared to be pulling a wagon filled with small logs of wood. Another gnome sat in a tiny swing, swaying slightly so that he looked almost alive.

As Charley leaned on the wall and stared into the garden, she discovered more and more gnomes, some grouped around a miniature well, one winding the windlass, others apparently gardening with rakes and watering cans. A countryside of gnomes. They were grotesque rather than beautiful. No two were alike but they were all so different from the usual garden ornament that she could only suppose their owner had collected them from some foreign country, and set them down here to remind him of his travels.

She moved toward the gate. Her mouth was so dry now that she could scarcely swallow. Someone with a garden full of toys should be easier to approach for a drink of water than someone with a garden full of tidy geraniums, she thought. The low door was ajar, and as she hesitated, giving a husky little cough rather than a knock, an old man suddenly put his head out and glared at her.

"*Now* what do you want?" he demanded in a high, rasping voice.

"Please can I have—" began Charley.

"No, you can't," said the old man, and disappeared again.

Charley stared at the gnomes and wondered what to do. He had not even waited to hear what she wanted. A moment later his head shot out again.

"What are you waiting for?" he shouted. "I won't sell any of 'em, I told you that afore, so it ain't no use

49

for you to keep coming worrying." He stopped and peered at her. "Ah, so you're another one, are you? What do *you* want, then?" His voice was still sharply suspicious.

"Please could I have a drink of water? I'm so thirsty—I—" To her surprise Charley found she was almost crying. Perhaps because the old man was being so unpleasant, perhaps because her own voice—which she had scarcely heard since she had said good-bye to Aunt Emm all those hours ago—sounded so strangely forlorn and far away. The garden swam in front of her eyes. It was beginning to feel like a bright, horrible dream . . . all those gnomes . . . She gave a small dry sob which turned into a hiccup, and the old man gave her one short, exasperated glance, then turned indoors.

But a moment later he was back again with a battered tin mug full of water, which he handed to her. Charley drained it almost at one gulp, and came up gasping and grateful.

"That was gorgeous. Thank you awfully!" Her voice sounded more like her own again.

"More?" She nodded, and he went to refill the mug.

"Do you know," she said to him earnestly, when the second mugful was nearly gone, "I think that was *the* nicest water I ever tasted."

The old man looked almost pleased. "That'll be because you was dry. That's what that'll be," he said.

"Yes—well, partly," said Charley. "But it *is* specially nice water. I'd love to take some away. Could I?"

He became suddenly suspicious again. "You wouldn't be making a game of me, would you?"

"No. I really mean it," said Charley. "It *is* lovely water, and look—I've got a bottle—" she held it out to him. "*Please* could you fill it?"

He shook his head. "I ain't never seen nothing so special in it meself," he said disbelievingly. "It comes out of a tap, same as most other water do these days. Still, water don't cost nothing—" He took the bottle from her and went indoors again. "Now, when I were a lad, it were diffcrent," he shouted from inside. "We didn't have no taps then."

Charley moved nearer the door. "I haven't got a tap where I live," she said, hoping this might explain things.

"Is that a fact now?" The old man appeared again suddenly, with a surprised look on his face. "I thought we was all on the mains now, since Michaelmas. Ain't you got the sewage neither, then?"

Charley thought it safer to change the subject. "I like your garden. Where did they all come from?"

"Made 'em," he said. "Made 'em all meself. Took me a rare-little-old-while, that lot did."

"*Did* you? All of them?" Charley was amazed. "But what did you make them out of?"

"Any old bits and pieces. Just whatever I might find laying about the place."

"I thought you must have got them from abroad," said Charley. "I thought they must have cost an awful lot of money."

"Bah!" The old man was looking quite pleased now. "*I* ain't never been abroad. *Nor* had no money."

"I've never been abroad either," said Charley. "Some of the girls at school are going to Spain for a *proper* holiday. They're lucky."

"Bah!" he said again. He leaned forward and wagged a finger at her. "Now you listen to me, my lass. It ain't what you've got nor where you go what counts. It's what you do with what you've got, wherever you happens to be."

"Oh," said Charley, "that sounded rather good. Would you mind saying it again?"

The old man repeated it. "It ain't what you've got nor where you go what counts. It's what you do with what you've got, wherever you happens to find yourself."

"You said 'happens to be' last time," said Charley.

"Did I? Well, it makes no odds. Same meat, different gravy. And any road, what do *you* mean, standing there and contradicting an old man like that? I'll it say whatever way I chooses. Now go you along back where you come from, and don't you come back neither, d'you hear?"

"I'm sorry," said Charley, "I just thought it was good, what you said, and I wanted to get it right. I'll go now—"

"And don't you come back neither," the old man repeated.

"Good-bye," said Charley. "Thank you for the water"—she hesitated, wondering where she was to get the next lot from—"I'll try not to come back."

"That's right." He nodded, looking suddenly almost kind. "Now you remember, I don't never want to see you no more, see? You be a good lass and leave a poor old man alone, will you? That way we'll always keep friends without never bothering each other, see? Now be you gone. It be getting late."

He followed her down to the gate, and Charley, looking back to wave, saw him latching it carefully behind her. She hesitated for a moment in case he should look up, then saw that he was tying the latch firmly to the gatepost with a length of string.

6

Hen House Corner

The way back seemed shorter. Charley plodded along with the old man's words still running in her head until she found herself walking in time to them . . . *It ain't what you've got nor where you go what counts, it's what you do with what you've got, wherever you happens to be. It ain't what you've got* . . . and so on. On and on.

"Oh, stop it!" she said at last, and changing her step to alter the rhythm, she thought instead about Auntie Louie, whether she was back from work yet, and how long it would be before anyone realized she had run away.

As she neared the end of the cart track, she felt a sudden urge to have a closer look at Holmdene before finally turning her back on it. She walked carefully on, looking sharply about, and came out at the top of Bell Lane. The road was empty.

Holmdene was a prim, clean council house with a small tidy garden and a green painted gate. The concrete path went straight up to the front door. There was no sign of life about, but she remembered this was usual; the front of the house had always had a blind look, its windows closed and covered with net curtains. She stood looking, and thinking how odd it was that Auntie Louie should live in a house so entirely unlike herself. It had a thin, mean, secret look about it, whereas Auntie Louie was fat, and generous, and talkative. It looked uninviting and unwelcoming. But then, Auntie Louie had not turned out to be so very welcoming either . . .

Nothing—nothing short of deluge or earthquake, thought Charley, would make her walk up that short concrete path and knock on the door. But it was nice to know it was there. Just in case. In case of earthquake or deluge, that was. She turned back to the cart track, scrambled through the hedge, and ran out into the field.

Back in her hen house corner the shadows had lengthened and it looked even more hidden away. She set about arranging her bed before the sun should get too low. Under the tree it should be, in case it rained. She scooped out a shallow trough in the soft earth with her hands, and marked the four

corners with sticks. Mosquitoes zoomed about her
ears and stung her legs as she worked, and a wood
pigeon complained ceaselessly from a distant copse—
"Oh my poor *toe*, Betty. Oh my poor *toe*, Betty!"

"Oh, shut up!" said Charley, busily gathering
leaves to fill the hollow of her bed. "Who cares about
your toe?"

The wood pigeon stopped abruptly. She glanced
up, startled. But a moment later the bubbling com-
plaint began again and she was relieved. At least it
was companionable—like Toby when he was lying
awake, grizzling because he had toothache.

When she had filled the hollow with as many
leaves as she could find, she spread out her mackintosh on top for a groundsheet. That would have to do.
She lay down on it to try it out, and looked up into
the green canopy of leaves over her head, layer upon
layer of them, going right up into the heart of the
tree. It was a lot better than the pattern of cracks on
the bedroom ceiling at home. Just staring up into all
that greenness made you feel good—and drowsy—and
—well, better altogether. How lucky she was! She
could be like Titania now—Titania, queen of the
fairies, sleeping out in her woodland bower . . . or a
gypsy, perhaps . . . or was she just homeless—like
Lizzie Scrotton?

She sprang up again quickly. Anyway that was her
bed settled. It was a bit hard but later she would

hope to find more leaves, or perhaps some straw. She had no blanket, but she would sleep in her thickest clothes, jeans and a roll-neck jersey. And she would wear her pajamas underneath to make it feel more right.

Now it was time for supper. She found that earwigs had already discovered the food in the hen house. She brushed them off, then, still eating, arranged a new larder by hanging the basket from a bough of the tree, and tying it with the belt of her hated green dress.

She rearranged the shelves in the hen house, laid out her brush and comb to make it look more home-like, and put the book she had brought with her on the bed (in case she should want to read in the morning).

Now what she needed was a table, and something to sit on if the grass should be really wet. She had seen an old wooden box lying under the hedge on her way up to the cart track. She went to fetch it. That was her table. On a pile of rubbish behind one of the outhouses she found an empty potted meat jar and a battered old bucket, heavy with dried cement. She dragged it back. Turned upside down it was just the thing for a stool, and only slightly wobbly. The potted meat jar, of course, was a flower vase.

Playing at houses like this, finding makeshift furniture, and deciding where things should go was all part of an old, familiar game—a game Charley had played often enough and always enjoyed. She was enjoying it now, but all the while she was being so busy she was also quietly frightened inside. She kept herself occupied as long as she could, trying not to notice that the wood pigeon had gone quiet, and the noise of the stacking machine had stopped, and the sun had moved away out of her corner.

At last she stopped, and stood still.

"It's no good you being afraid of a silly little thing like sleeping out alone," she told herself sternly. "I should think it's a far more frightening thing (a far beastlier thing, anyway) to go on living with someone who hates you, or to go and stay with someone who's specially said they don't want you." And this helped to whip up her anger again. She found that when she was hurt and angry, she forgot to be afraid, so several times, as the sun moved farther over and the shadows under the hedge grew darker, she deliberately reminded herself how hateful everyone had been, and how justly they would be punished when they discovered she had run away.

At dusk she knew it was bedtime. She changed into her pajamas and put on her jersey and jeans. An owl flapped by, close over her head. "Silly great thing," she whispered furiously, "those are only homemade wings—anyone can see that. You can't frighten me." But she was glad when it had lumbered away over the hedge and disappeared into the darkness. She lay down on her bed and pulled her duffel coat up around her. But as soon as she closed her eyes, she was wide awake. All the happenings of the day passed through her mind like pictures. Aunt Emm at the coach station, waving the labels, the old man with the gnomes, Holmdene, looking so grim and unwelcoming . . .

By now Auntie Louie would be home again. It was comforting to know she was there. It made all the difference, especially now when the dark tree above her was creaking slightly, and twigs snapped suddenly, and small things rustled in the grass. She closed her eyes again and tried to imagine what the Hewitts would be doing now. Something light fluttered down onto her face and she sat up in sudden fright. It was only a leaf but, once sitting up, she found she dared not lie down again.

It was no good; she could not sleep here tonight. Should she, after all, pack up and go around there? They would be wondering why she had not arrived. If she turned up on the doorstep at this late hour—perhaps with some story about the bus having broken down—surely they would be awfully relieved and glad to see her? Or would they? Perhaps by now they would be expecting her to come tomorrow instead. In

any case—*I don't want Charley. You know that . . .*
Again she remembered the hateful sentence. Nothing
would induce her to go around to Auntie Louie's.

Nevertheless, she could not stay here. She got up,
put on her coat, and felt her way along the hedge
until she came to the place where she used to creep
through last year. She dropped down into the far end
of the Hewitts' garden. Immediately, she felt on
familiar ground and was relieved.

A cluster of sheds and piles of wood blocked the
view of the back of the house. She crept as far as the
apple tree and looked around. Yes, the house was
still there! There was no light in the scullery, and
that was the only window where she might have
expected to see one. That meant they had finished
washing up, and were watching television in the
front room.

Limp with relief, and suddenly very tired, Charley
crept back behind the shed and lay down with her
back against the wall. The Hewitts would never
know she was here, but if she really needed them
(only in case of earthquake or deluge, she reminded
herself), she could be up at the house in less than a
minute.

She stared up at the black branches of the chestnut tree, moving slightly against the sky, and the
stars that appeared and disappeared among its
leaves. It was strange how different it felt, just being

the other side of the hedge. Now she felt really at home . . . Her eyelids grew heavy. The stars and the branches swam together, and in another moment she was asleep.

7

A Dumb Girl

Charley stirred. She was aware of the whisper and rustle of leaves, and the cool night air on her face, but they were like part of a dream. It might be frightening if she really woke up—she could not remember why—and still wrapped around in the warmth of sleep, she sank down into unconsciousness again.

It was dawn when she woke properly. The sky was lightening and the air was full of the twitter of birds. She sprang up and scrambled through the hedge, which was hung with great glistening spiders' webs. A ground mist lay over the field. She sat on her bed now wet with dew, and hugged her knees.

I've done it! she thought. *I've run away, and I've slept out alone all night!* And she could hardly believe it.

She dressed, and ate a piece of Mrs. Scrotton's dough cake for breakfast, and finished the water she had brought back last night. *Now I must make sensible plans*, she thought. *I need water, and something to carry it in, and food . . .* She looked to see what was left. Half the dough cake, and the box of chocolates. She ate her ration of two chocolates while thinking what she must buy. Bread. And cheese. Eggs were no good, they would need cooking. So would sausages. But there was always corned beef. And a bottle of milk—and fruit. She would need a tin opener too. And what about a mug and spoon, if there was enough money?

She sat writing a list until the sun was well up and the mist had cleared. Then she wrapped the food in her mackintosh and stowed it away in the hen house, along with all her other things. Then, with her purse and shopping list and basket, she set off across the fields in the direction of the main road.

She was going to avoid Market Barnham altogether by cutting across the fields toward Brinchester, two or three miles along the road. Fortunately she remembered Auntie Louie often took a bus from the bottom of Bell Lane along to Welston, five miles in the opposite direction. No doubt that would also be where she was working. There would be nothing for her to do in a little village like Brinchester.

There was a fresh, early-morning smell in the air,

when the time came to pay, laid out her money on the counter and let the woman take the correct amount herself.

"There you are, me dear," said the woman—she pronounced the word "dear" like "dare"—"There you are, me dare, and there's something extra for yourself," and she put a bar of nougat in on top of the oranges.

Charley opened her mouth to say thank you,

remembered just in time, and bowed her head in grateful acknowledgment instead. Then she picked up her things and ran. It had worked perfectly. Rather too well, in fact. She felt a little guilty about the nougat, which she knew she had come by unfairly. Perhaps she would post it to Toby later on.

At an ironmonger's she bought a small plastic bucket, and a plastic mug, plate and spoon. Also a tin opener. Here, too, she used sign language, but as the old man who served her was very slow and very deaf, her own dumbness passed unnoticed. Clearly he was used to people waving their arms about and pointing to what they wanted.

She also bought a large bottle of orange squash which would hold her drinking water. She would pour half the orange into her small lemonade bottle, and fill this one up with water—when she could find some. It would mean she could not have any plain water until she had finished the orangeade, but she could not imagine that would be any hardship. Would it be better to brush her teeth in orangeade or not at all? She could not decide.

It was a relief at last to leave the village behind her. Out on the open road she sang loudly for the pleasure of hearing her own voice again, and decided she would only be dumb when she went shopping.

She drank half the carton of milk, sitting on the grass by the roadside, and ate a hunk of bread torn from the crisp new loaf. It tasted delicious. The sun blazed down, burning her bare arms and legs, and a skylark trilled, higher and higher, somewhere far above her head. She was happy, with a fierce, triumphant kind of happiness. She had run away, and was making a proper job of it. How surprised Giles would be if he could see her now!

8

The Man in Brown

But water, that was the problem.

The carton of milk was finished, and Charley was still thirsty by the time she got back. Somewhere she must find a tap near enough to use every day and yet not so near that her hiding place would be discovered. She hid her shopping in the hen house and, taking only the partially emptied bottle of orange squash, went in search of water once more.

She followed along the hedge at the far side of the field, well away from the backs of the houses and gardens in Bell Lane, peering through the sparser branches below, until she came to a gap. Here she stopped.

A long garden lay on the other side—rows and rows of vegetables stretching away down a slope. Lower

down there were fruit trees, one or two small sheds
and a greenhouse. And beyond that, a clump of tall,
dark trees with a gable and chimneys rising above
them. Away to her right a rough narrow path ran
down the side of the garden, and here she saw
something that made her heart lift. A long, green
garden hose, winding, snakelike, away down the
path.

And where there was a hose there must be a tap!

Cautiously Charley crawled through the gap and picked her way between cabbages out onto the path. Nobody seemed to be about, but she must be careful. She walked gingerly down the garden, following the hose, and looking along the hedge, which was covered with a mass of sprawling convolvulus, for the tap which she knew must be there. At the bottom of

the slope, beyond the greenhouse, she could now see clusters of bright flowers, and a white gate leading out onto the road.

She was already halfway down when a man came suddenly around the corner of the greenhouse. She stood stock-still, hardly daring to breathe and counting up to twenty quickly under her breath, while she tried to decide what to do. Then, in a kind of despair, she sat down on the ground and stared earnestly at a patch of moss, waiting for the worst to happen.

The tramping steps grew louder, then stopped, and a pair of large muddy boots appeared on the path in front of her.

"Oh, ay, what's this? Tired of waiting, eh?" said a deep, husky voice. "You shoulda come around ten, like they mostly does. I goes to me lunch at half after."

Charley looked up. A man with a wrinkled red-brown face, wearing a brown cap, a brown waistcoat, and brown baggy trousers tied around with string, was looking down at her. Everything about him seemed to be brown, even his eyes.

"You're new 'round here, ain't you?" he said. "I don't remember you coming afore."

Charley scrambled to her feet, hot with relief. "No, I haven't been before," she said.

"Oh, ay, I thought not. What was you wanting,

then? There's kale, cabbage, beans—not many peas, them-down-there's wanting *them,* of course." He jerked his head down the slope. "Where's your basket?"

Charley shook her head. "I didn't come for anything, really—"

"Just to pass the time of day, eh? Folks often does that—pops in to say good morning. Who told you about me?"

"Nobody. I just came—I was just looking—" she licked her dry lips. Beyond his shoulder, farther along the hedge, she had just seen the tap. "Would you mind if I filled this up with water? It's too strong to drink as it is, and I'm rather thirsty." She held up the bottle of orange squash.

"Go on, help yourself. But turn the tap off after you."

She followed him down the path, trying not to look too eager, and while she filled the bottle, he went on down the garden and began picking peas. Charley ducked her head quickly, and drank and drank. Then, with her chin still dripping, she walked down toward him. Somehow she must ask if she could come again, without arousing suspicion. He was halfway along the row and seemed not to notice her. She waited.

"You come a long way, then?" he asked suddenly, not looking up.

"Oh, yes—quite," said Charley.

"I never see'd you come in," he said. "Funny that. I was in the greenhouse when I come back from lunch. I shoulda seen you go by."

Charley said quickly, "I came in at the top end, through the hedge. I hope you don't mind. It—it would have been a long way round by the road."

"Ah, you come from up the Bell, eh?"

"You mean Bell Lane? Well, yes—at least—" she hesitated. "Not *in* Bell Lane. Farther away."

"Oh, ay, more Thornley way."

Thornley was the village beyond, over the hill, where the old man with the gnomes lived. Charley did not contradict him. "Shall I help you with those?" she asked. "I like picking peas."

"That'd be kind. Then I can get on with them sprouts. Got the blight, they have." He handed her the basket and went trudging up to the top of the garden.

This was wonderful, thought Charley, walking slowly along the rows picking the peas, and eating the young, tender ones as she went. He had not minded her coming through the hedge, and he seemed to take her presence in the garden for granted. She wondered who the others were who mostly came around ten. It sounded as though he was used to people coming in to buy vegetables.

She crammed her mouth with the young peas,

juicy and sweet, thinking how *real* this was—to be seizing her food surreptitiously, wherever she could find it. She longed to tell someone, to show off a little, but knew it would be dangerous.

"Do you sell apples?" she asked when she carried the basket back, full.

"Oh, ay." He straightened his back and pointed down to the fruit trees. "Or maybe there's some windfalls down there you could have for nothing. Go you on down and have a look. Mind the wasps in 'em, though."

Charley scrabbled about in the grass under the fruit trees and found five or six apples, some half rotten, some nearly whole. She ate the better parts of the rotten ones and ran back with the others in her hand. "I found some!" she said, holding them out for him to see.

"That's good," he said, not bothering to look up.

"I'll tell you why I wanted them," she said, casually, still longing to share her secret. "I wanted them to eat."

He glanced up at her, grinning. "Well, now, I thought maybe you did."

"No, I mean I was getting hungry. I ate some of your peas as well while I was picking them."

He seemed unimpressed. "Ay, they's good when they's young and sweet, they is. Them-down-there cooks 'em," he added with disgust.

"As a matter of fact I've run away," said Charley, suddenly throwing caution to the winds. "That's why I was hungry."

He did not look nearly surprised enough. "Have you, now? All the way from Thornley, eh?" His eyes twinkled. "And where would you be living now, then?"

Charley was silent, wondering how much she dared to tell him.

"Down the bottom of the garden, maybe?" he said, still teasing her, and she realized that whatever she said, he would only think it was a game.

He must have noticed her disappointed look. He stopped smiling and said seriously, "There now, you don't want to take no notice of me. What's the harm if you/wants to be off on your own for a bit? Only don't let your Ma get worried, staying out too long, will you? Terrible creatures for worrying, women are."

"Oh, no, I wouldn't!" said Charley. "But my mother's away, you see. My auntie's looking after us—me—while she's away."

He nodded understandingly. "Oh, ay! And aunties ain't never the same. That I do know. Well, come again tomorrow if you like, and maybe I can find some more apples for you to eat in your little old hideout. Make sure they're ripe, though. Auntie won't thank me if you gets the bellyache, come nighttimes, will she?" He laughed—a rich, deep, brown-colored laugh, it seemed to Charley. "And I won't tell on you, that's a promise!" he added.

He turned back to the sprouts again, and Charley felt it was time to go. But that had been very satisfactory. The windfalls would help to eke out her own money. She might even live on them when it ran out. Or eat raw vegetables. But best of all was the tap. She could fetch her water every day, and if he would let her help him in the garden, that would be a secret way of paying for it.

9

Where a Fawn Might Live

The hen house corner looked very green and quiet and familiar when Charley got back to it, and she wondered that she had been afraid of sleeping there last night. Now it was where she lived.

She was not sure of the time, but it felt like afternoon. Had she had lunch or not? The snack by the roadside would count as elevenses, she decided. So would the peas and the apples she had eaten in the garden. She was hungry again, so it must be lunchtime. The earwigs had started on the bread and cheese already—she had forgotten to hang the basket up. She shook them off, wishing she had thought of buying a tin. But that would have cost too much. A plastic bag would be the answer. She must buy one this afternoon.

She ate another hunk off the loaf, with a piece of cheese, and washed it down with a drink of orangeade. What were the others doing now? she wondered. In another few days Toby and Aunt Emm would be leaving for Southsea. Giles would be going to the Barretts the evening before. Auntie Louie had no telephone, so when Charley did not turn up today, she would probably write a letter asking Aunt Emm what had happened. But by the time the letter arrived Aunt Emm might have gone. How long did it take for a letter to be forwarded? One day—two? At any rate, as long as she kept out of the Hewitts' way, she would have three whole days to herself. Three days in which to go where she liked, do what she liked, even be who she liked. After that she would have to be more careful. They would know she was lost then, and start looking for her. They might even get the police . . .

The sun blazed down into her camp and the wood pigeon burbled in the distance. She lay down on her bed under the tree and looked up into the layers of green leaves. Now would have been the time to write her diary, she thought, so much seemed to have happened in the last two days. But she had given it to Toby. Bother. And yet, when she closed her eyes and thought about it, the things that had happened were more like pictures. They were things you would paint rather than write about. "Went to Thornley" meant nothing, but someone going up that long cart track (had it really been only yesterday?), with the stones showing white through the tufts of grass, and the birds flying up, black, out of the hedges, and the sky huge and bright blue overhead—that was like a picture. A picture of someone going from nowhere to nowhere. . .

She remembered her paint box and sat up. But she had no paint water. Bother again! Never mind, there was plenty of time. Tomorrow she would fetch more water. In any case, she must buy a plastic bag first or the earwigs would finish up all the food.

She went by way of the copse. It was a longer way around, but when she left the little wood she could easily cut back to the road again. The intermittent cooing of the wood pigeon grew louder as she came nearer, then ceased. But as she went in among the trees, a large bird rose up in front of her with a great flapping of wings, and flew up onto a branch with a throaty bubble of protest.

"Oh, it's you!" said Charley, startled. "How's your toe?"

She went on in, pushing aside nettles and bracken, and found herself in a place so quiet, so enclosed that she only had to tread on a twig and it sounded like a pistol shot. A mossy path led away between silver birches. Birds flew ahead of her, swooping from branch to branch. A rabbit sat perfectly still, as if petrified, under a bush, and then darted away with a streak of white tail.

This was a magic place, she thought. The sort of place where her fawn might live. Where it could dance on the springy moss, lie down to rest in the bracken, or run for cover between the trees if it heard her coming . . . She walked on quietly, glancing to left and right, almost as if she really expected to see a fawn looking out at her from under the silvery, shivery leaves. This was where it would dance on a moonlight night, she thought, coming to a small round patch of green turf . . .

It was funny how she always thought of the fawn as dancing—how Giles would have laughed if he had known! Charley could not dance. She was too self-conscious and always imagined she looked foolish. She had endured one dreadful term of dancing classes, going with Giles when they were much younger, and the memory of it still made her go hot all over. Giles had been all right in his buckled shoes and velvet shorts, with his solemn face. But she, in a silly little tunic with frills on it, had not been all right at all. How could one pretend to be a butterfly or a flower fairy on that dreadful slippery floor with everyone looking?

So Charley had given up going to dancing. And her fawn danced for her instead . . .

She could not remember when she had first

81

thought of the fawn—probably she had read about it first in a fairy tale—but gradually she had come to think of this particular fawn—the one she was always trying to draw—as if it were her own. When she was little, she had owned an imaginary horse. A horse that, miraculously, could gallop her home in next to no time when she was tired, on some long, dreary walk. But the fawn was different. Never useful to her, it was just an idea, a thought, too difficult to put into words, but in her own mind a sign for everything that was magical, secret, and beautiful. It had nothing to do with ordinary things, like school, or family, or home. It lived in a world of its own. So now, when Charley was wandering away from all those ordinary things, drowsy with sunshine and dreamy with lack of sleep, she would hardly have been surprised to see it come tripping out of the undergrowth to meet her . . .

Out again in the sunbaked field, she decided not to go to Brinchester this time, but to try one of the smaller villages instead. A short way along the main road she turned off at a signpost, and down a lane.

In the first village, she came on an old church surrounded by trees, a few cottages, but no shop of any kind. She trudged on, and the dusty lane brought her out onto a stretch of open road. It was so hot in the full glare of the sun that the tar had melted in places and stuck to her sneakers. She sat

down on the grass and took them off, surprised to see
how white her feet looked compared to her legs and
arms, which were already a reddish-brown color and
covered with scratches and bruises.

She picked a bunch of the wild flowers growing
beside her and made them into a necklace, daisy-
chain fashion. She was like a girl in a picture, she
thought—sitting barefooted, with flowers in her lap;
and she saw herself, and the grass, and the fields
beyond as if they were all enclosed in a frame. She
pondered dreamily over suitable titles—"Girl with
Flowers," "Summer Day," or just "Norfolk Scene"—
and when a car suddenly flashed by, she hoped the
people inside it had seen her in the same way—as
part of the country picture.

It was farther than she had thought to the next
village. By the time it came in sight she was no
longer a girl in a picture, but Charley—dusty, dry,
and footsore, with a string of withered flowers hanging around her neck. On the outskirts of the village
she saw a girl coming toward her, sucking an iced
lolly. It was just what she needed. "Where did you
get that from?" she asked her as she was passing.

The girl stopped, and stared. "I bought it. From
the van."

"Where is it now?"

The girl waved a hand vaguely. "Gone now. Over
Barnham way, I should think."

"Is there anywhere round here I could buy one?"

The girl shook her head, looking at her curiously. "Where you come from? I ain't seen you here before."

"I haven't been here before."

"Oh. Where d'you live, then?"

"Miles away," said Charley. "Under a tree." The

girl stared at her unbelievingly. "It's true. I live under a tree—by myself—and I've got a hen house for a wardrobe." (Charley was brightening up.)

The girl's eyes widened. "What d'you live on, then?"

"Raw peas, rotten apples, anything I can find. Where can I buy a plastic bag?"

"What you want a plastic bag for?" The girl was looking at her suspiciously now.

"The earwigs are eating my bread," said Charley. "Such a nuisance."

"You serious?"

"Perfectly serious." Charley flung out an arm casually. "I live on my own, you see. I've run away. Is there a shop down there?"

The girl nodded. She was really impressed now. "Bor! Ain't they looking for you? Ain't you scared?"

"Not really. There's nothing to it." Charley waved an airy hand and went on down into the village.

10

Lest a Bird Enter and Die of Thirst

In the one little general shop she became a dumb
girl again. But this time it was not so easy. The man
who served her looked at her with mistrust, and she
found it impossible to describe a plastic bag without
speaking. At last she wrote the word "bag" on the
counter with her finger, and he produced a packet of
greaseproof paper bags. She did not like to argue, and
paid for them. In answer to her spelling out "milk"
on the counter and making signs that she wanted
something to drink, he merely shook his head and
said, "All gone."

As she left the shop, she saw him wiping the
counter where she had touched it, as if it might have
become contaminated in some way. She would certainly not go there again! He had looked at her as if
she were some sort of tramp. But what about Lizzie
Scrotton? Might people have looked at her like that?
The idea had not occurred to her before.

She plodded back the way she had come, glancing sideways into cottage windows as she passed, always hoping she might see the same things as Lizzie Scrotton had seen so long ago. But no old ladies were

sitting in front of their fires, no children were sitting up to tea around a table. One old lady, standing at her door, disappeared inside when she saw her coming, and as Charley passed, she saw the curtains at the tiny window twitch, and the old lady's pale face staring out at her between the potted plants.

The only children she saw were three little girls in crisp cotton dresses and white socks, who were taking turns riding a tricycle. One of them sniggered as she went by, and Charley, realizing she was still wearing the necklace of wild flowers, held up her head and minced along with an air of elegant disdain, defying them to notice that they were really dead weeds. (If they couldn't recognize a garland of flowers when they saw one, more fools they.) Around the next corner she dropped the withered necklace on the side of the road and trudged on.

By the time she arrived back at the first village she was so hot and thirsty that all the joy had gone out of the afternoon. She turned into the churchyard and sat for a while in the shade under the trees. No one else was about, and nothing disturbed the long-ago quietness of the place. The only sound was of rooks cawing in the elms. The gravestones around her were very old, some of them tilted sideways and half-hidden in the long grass. She made out the date on the one nearest to her. It was 1832.

Lizzie Scrotton would have seen that, she thought, *if she'd been sitting where I'm sitting now. And if it was summertime, she'd have had blisters, like me, and been longing for a drink . . .*

She got up and hobbled over to the church. The door was shut and there was a notice fixed to it, which read:

> *Of your charity*
> *Pray latch these doors*
> *Lest a bird enter*
> *And die of thirst.*

A sudden sadness came over Charley. Oh, poor little bird, she thought. And poor dead people with your gravestones all crooked. And poor, poor Lizzie, with your blisters, and nowhere to live . . . and she felt a stinging behind her eyelids, and wept for the sadness of everything—quite forgetting that the unknown bird might never have died of thirst, and the unknown dead would never know their headstones were crooked, and that Lizzie Scrotton was long since grown up and grown old, living perfectly happily on a chicken farm outside Royston.

An hour later, back in her hen house corner, Charley had forgotten her sadness. She was, after all, so much luckier than Lizzie Scrotton. Here she had all she needed. A long drink of orangeade, a place to sleep, and her own things about her (some of them, anyway), and a world away—yet only the other side of the hedge—Auntie Louie, and safety.

How astonished the Hewitts would be if they knew she had been living here all this time! She would not have dared if they had not been there. It would have been an awful thing to do, dangerous, as well as frightening. But knowing she could break the spell at any minute simply by turning up on the doorstep, made all the difference.

For supper she had the small tin of corned beef—which proved surprisingly difficult to open—and the other half of the dough cake, which had been wrapped up in her mackintosh all day and tasted of rubber. After that, she sat sucking an orange, watching the sky turn gradually pinker, and wondering how she was going to keep awake until bedtime. Her eyelids were heavy after being out in the fresh air all day, and her legs and face burned. But she dared not lie down on her bed in case she fell asleep while it was still light. There was always the possibility that someone might come along and find her there if she did not keep a sharp lookout. A soft haze was coming down over the distant fields, but it would not be dusk for another hour or more. She got up, cleared away her few supper things, and went back across the field toward the copse.

Now that the sun had gone from all but the tops of the trees, it seemed even more secluded, and secret, and magical. She tiptoed down the mossy path, farther than she had gone that afternoon, coming at last to a clearing where the ground sloped upward in front of her. At the top was a rowan tree, its upper branches laden with orange-red berries, still touched by the sun. The tree glowed as if it were on fire. Fascinated by its brilliance, Charley climbed the slope. *My tree*, she thought, and sat down under it.

There was a soft, rushing sound in the leaves overhead—like the sound of water, or fine summer rain. But it was not rain, only a slight breeze stirring the fine, feathery leaves of the rowan. She slipped down in the grass and lay listening to the soothing, whispering sound, and gradually her eyes closed.

Charley slept, and in her sleep she heard the sound of music—a horn, or was it a flute?—playing a thin, strange little tune, both sweet and sad. A wandering tune, with a phrase that repeated itself, of little notes running downhill, then up again; like someone running a few steps, then pausing, then running back . . .

The music drifted through the copse, wandered around the clearing, grew louder for a moment, then died away in the tops of the trees. Charley awoke with the sound of it still in her ears. Then there was silence. The tune went on in her head, but there was no sound except the whisper of the leaves overhead and the distant lowing of a cow. She got to her feet and stumbled in the half-light back to her camp.

Making her bed under the chestnut tree, she tried to remember the tune, but it eluded her. She wondered if she had been dreaming, but if so, she was dreaming now, because she remembered so clearly having heard it. She lay down, pulling up her duffel coat around her, and her last muddled thought before falling asleep was that she had washed her face in dew that morning, and perhaps it was something to do with that.

11

In Ned's Garden

Charley was in the garden again early next morning. In fact she had been lying under the hedge for quite a while before she saw the man in brown moving about by the greenhouse; then she went down to meet him. He was hanging his jacket over the handles of the wheelbarrow, and turned around in surprise when she greeted him.

"Hallo! How're you going on, eh? All right?"

"Yes, thank you."

"All right, eh? That's good." He took a fork and started up the path towards the vegetable rows. Charley followed him. "You're up early, ain't you? Don't your auntie give you no breakfast, then?" he asked, not turning round.

"Yes, I've had it," said Charley, smiling. She had—

two apples and two chocolates, and a hunk of bread
she had shared with a blackbird.

"Oh, ay, that's good." He bent down and began
pulling up corncobs. "She goes to work, then, do
she?" he asked, not looking up.

Charley nodded. "In Welston," she said, adding
under her breath, "I think."

"Oh, ay. I thought that might be it." He worked
his way along the row, and she stood watching.

"You sounds bright enough, any road," he said to
the corncobs.

"Oh yes, I am!"

He straightened up and looked her up and down,
then grinned broadly. "Ain't had yer bath yet, I see.
Saturday nights, is it?"

Charley looked down at herself. She had not noticed before how dirty she was. She wondered about
her face.

"I did wash," she said, remembering the cool
splashing of the long dewy grass in the early morning. (But she had forgotten to buy soap. That was a
nuisance!)

"I've come to help you—if you like," she said. "I've
brought a bucket of my own to put the peas in—if
you want some more picked, that is." Cunningly, she
had decided not to mention yet that the bucket was
really for water. It would be easy enough to rinse it
under the tap after she had emptied it, and then just
happen to fill it up with water again before leaving.

He was happy to be helped. That was tidily kind
of her, he said. Them-down-there was wanting a rare
old load this morning—French beans as well as the
corncobs, and no one but him to do the picking of
them. "That's the trouble," he said, "there ain't nobody nowhere to help with nothing—not now young
Barry's on holiday."

This was just what Charley liked to hear. As they

picked the beans together, she learned gradually that his name was Edward Bunn but people mostly called him Ned, and that he—with young Barry to help him—was gardener for them-down-there at the big house among the trees, which she gathered was a guest house.

"And what's your name?" he asked.

Charley hesitated. There was the remote possibility of his meeting Auntie Louie and hearing she had lost a girl called Charley. But apart from that she did not want to be called Charley now. Not here. She need not be Charley the funny (as she frequently was at school), or Charley the surly (as she more frequently was at home). She could be who she liked.

"My name's Rowan," she said, with a kind of quiet dignity.

"Ah, that's a pretty name," he said. "That's the name of a tree, that is."

"I know."

As they worked their way along the rows of beans, Ned became more talkative, and Charley learned quite a lot without having to ask too many questions. She discovered that he regarded the garden entirely as his own, and that his greatest trial was having to gather large quantities of his precious vegetables every morning for the people in the guest house to eat. "That ain't natural, not to my way of thinking," he said in his gentle, grumbling voice, looking sadly at the pile of beans already in his basket. "They ain't never got no need to eat all that lot. Not every day, they ain't. Windy, any road, I'd a' thought."

But for the others—those who mostly came around ten—it was different. They were people from the village, who came to buy whatever was left over after the guest house people had had theirs. They knew a good vegetable when they saw one. Nobody could never tell *them* that Ned's wasn't wholly better than any they could buy in a shop. Ned was pleased and proud to oblige them. There were one or two other people he was happy to oblige as well. Old Maudie Heyhoe, for instance, who couldn't come out foraging for herself no more. It was no trouble to take her a few things sometimes on his way home. She'd always been partial to a boiled onion with butter, had Maudie. And Mrs. Denning, who used to live in the village, but had moved now and lived over Thornley way—

Here Ned broke off and looked over the bean sticks at Charley.

"Now that's up your way, ain't it? So you'll be knowing Mrs. Denning, of course. A right nice woman, ain't she? One of the old sort. Maybe you could take her some of these here corncobs on your way back? She was asking for some last time I see'd her, and I said I'd send young Barry up with 'em as soon as they was ready. But being as he's on holiday, she ain't had none yet, so it'd be right kind if you could take 'em."

Charley was a little dismayed at this, but tried not to show it and hoped Ned would have forgotten by the time she left.

"Now go and find some more windfalls," he said at last, "and I'll take this lot down to keep 'em quiet," and he loaded the vegetables on the barrow and trundled it away down the slope toward the house.

Quickly Charley rinsed her bucket under the tap, filled it with water, and left it by the gap in the hedge. Then she went down to collect apples and have a cautious look around the garden. The ground near the greenhouse was littered with flowerpots, piles of potatoes, a garden cultivator, and boxes of seedlings set out in rows. There was an orderly disorder about the place which made it seem homelike. She picked her way over the hose, now coiled on the path, and sniffed at the sweet peas which sprawled untidily over the trellis by the potting shed. A thrush flew up out of a clump of rhubarb and perched on the cultivator, watching her with a cautious, considering eye.

The sweet peas smelled unbelievably sweet. She wondered if she dared pick one or two to take away with her, then decided a few bean flowers were less likely to be missed. Anyway, they were the same color as the rowan berries in the copse. Lovely as Ned's garden was, the copse was better. It was her own, and her fawn lived there. As soon as she had taken her water back to hen house corner, she was going back there, to sit under her tree.

But Ned had not forgotten about the corncobs. As she started off up the path, she heard a shout and turned to see him coming after her with a cardboard box in his hands. She went back.

"Just tell her Ned Bunn sent 'em," he said, "and no need to pay till I sees her again. Her and me trusts each other. You know the house, don't you? In the trees, set back a bit. Past the Horseshoe, a little after old Garner's."

"Old Garner's?" Charley looked doubtful.

"Yes, old Lazarus Garner's, you know—"

Charley heard the gate click behind him. She did not want to be there when anyone from the village came. "What if she's out?" she asked quickly.

"Leave 'em by garden door," said Ned. "She'll know."

He turned away to see his first customer, and Charley crawled back through the hedge, and crossed the field with the box of corncobs under one arm, and the bucket of water in the other hand, trying not to slop too much over as she went. There would be time enough to take the corncobs up to Thornley later. First she would have a rest and something to eat. The day had barely begun as yet.

She covered the bucket of water with her mackintosh and hid it in the corner behind the chestnut tree. Then, with a lump of cheese and two windfalls to eat on the way, she went across to the copse.

Again the birds flew up with cries of alarm as she pushed her way through the bracken, and again she saw a rabbit scuttling away into the undergrowth. No matter how softly she walked, she felt like an intruder—a giant, blundering and crashing into the quietness of a small green world where nothing larger than a rabbit—or perhaps a fawn?—ever came.

She went through as far as the clearing and climbed the slope to the rowan tree, and there she sat down. There was still the soft rushing noise, sounding like water in the leaves, and she closed her eyes, listening—but this time there was no music, only the drone of insects.

She thought of her fawn—and behind closed eyelids, saw it come stepping delicately out of the undergrowth, lift its head to sniff the air, then run a few steps toward her across the clearing. It stopped, turning its head this way and that, and she held her breath, willing it to become real, willing it to come

99

nearer—near enough for her to touch. She felt the sharp sting of a mosquito bite on her hand, and opened her eyes.

The sunlight flicked down through the branches with dazzling brightness and made a moving pattern of light and shade on the grass. Even now, with her eyes open, she could not be sure she had not just seen some small brown creature dart across the clearing and away into the bracken . . .

12

Corncobs for Mrs. Denning

An hour later Charley was going up the long cart track once more, carrying the box of corncobs for Mrs. Denning. This time she hardly noticed the distance. Her thoughts were still in the copse, and it was only when she reached the cottage with the gnomes in the garden that she came out of her daydream. Then she paused to look over the wall.

At once the old man appeared in his doorway, his fist raised before he saw who it was. For a moment he stared, then let his hand drop, shook his head sorrowfully, and turned indoors again. Charley hurried on. She felt terrible about it, but there was nothing she could do. He had thought she was going to worry him again and there was no way of showing him she was not, except by going on quickly without a word. That way, he had said, they could always remain friends without bothering each other. He must have it his own way.

A little further on she discovered she had come too far after all. A woman beating a mat outside her cottage shook her head when Charley asked where the Horseshoe was. She pointed back over her shoulder.

"Way back, that is. You shoulda cut across the field afore Bartlett's."

"Bartlett's?"

"That's right. House with the garden—geraniums all set out nice. You musta passed it coming along. Lower down there's a footpath across to the Horseshoe. You'll see."

Charley thanked her and went back. As she passed the old man's cottage again, she saw out of the corner of her eye that he was still standing in his doorway. She quickened her pace and, without even looking at him, waved a hand, then broke into a run. Still waving, she ran on until she was well out of his sight, never once turning her head. That should show him.

She was halfway down the cart track when she found a break in the hedge and went through onto the footpath, passing the scarecrow on the way. Close up, it was a dreary-looking object, wearing an old man's jacket with great holes at the elbows, and the remains of what had once been a flowered dress underneath. "*You* need a new dress, Aunt Emm," said Charley.

She followed the footpath across to a distant clump of trees and came at last to the Horseshoe, a cobbled cottage with a painted sign hanging from its wall. She had now to find out where Lazarus Garner lived. She asked an old woman who was hobbling up the lane in bedroom slippers, carrying a pint of milk.

"Please can you tell me where Mr. Lazarus Garner lives?"

The old woman looked shocked. "Not nowhere, my maid. Dead he is. Dead twelve year come next muck raking." She looked curiously at Charley. "What was you wanting of him, then?"

"Can you tell me which was his house?"

"Old Garner's, where else? He never were a wanderer. Lived and died where he were born, Lazarus did."

"Could you show me where?" Charley asked patiently. The old woman jerked her head toward a derelict cottage on the other side of the lane. "That's the only Old Garner's *I* ever heared of," she said. "Who told you there was another?"

"Nobody," said Charley. "The name wasn't on it, that's why I asked."

"And what for should it want a name when everyone know where it is? That'd be a tidy waste of paint, that would."

Charley felt they were going around in circles so she resisted the temptation to answer back. She thanked her and went, leaving the old woman staring after her, shaking her head.

She came at last to some trees, and a long white gate. The trees bent over to make an archway down the drive, and at the far end Charley saw the corner of a white house. This must be Mrs. Denning's.

She crept quietly down the drive, looking warily about her, then tiptoed around the end of the house until she came to the garden. A smooth green lawn stretched in front of her, with a summerhouse at the far end, and a willow tree, and beyond that more trees. Down one side of the lawn ran a broad bed of brilliantly colored dahlias, and— Charley's heart jumped as she saw that an elderly woman with gray hair was bending over the border, snipping off the dead flower heads. Her back was turned.

Charley dropped the box of corncobs in the middle of the path, and ran. It would never do for her to be seen. She might be asked awkward questions about who she was, and where she lived. At the gate she remembered she had not left Ned's message, but it could not be helped. Anyway, Mrs. Denning *was* out. It was a pity she had not been even more out, Charley thought. Had there been a chance, she would have liked to stay longer, to explore the garden, perhaps look in the summerhouse, and walk the full length of that long, smooth lawn in her bare feet. There would have been no thorns or thistles there for sure. The short, velvety turf was a complete contrast to the rough grass round hen house corner. Even Ned's garden, which earlier had seemed so orderly and attractive, was really only a rough, overgrown sort of place, she realized, not much more than an allotment. But Mrs. Denning's had been like a garden in a picture.

She remembered her new paint box. Cool, and smooth, and shiny, it was still lying in its wrappings on the shelf in the hen house. She had paint water now—and the "refreshment" jar to put it in. She skipped the last few yards across the field, out on to the cart track, and ran back to hen house corner. The day was hers.

A distant cockcrow broke the silence of the after-noon. At last Charley stretched her legs, packed up her painting things, and put them away in the hen house. She would go for a walk. Eating a piece of bread and cheese as she went, she crossed the field, beyond Ned's garden, and skirted the copse. While she was still free to wander about, she would explore what lay on the farther side.

She passed a haystack and came to a field of stubble. Beyond that there seemed to be nothing after all, only more fields stretching away into the distance, and on the horizon, a church tower looking small and lost under the wide, empty sky. She turned back toward the copse, and came across a small caravan, nestling under a bank, half-hidden by bushes.

The door was open. She moved back a few steps, expecting someone to have heard her and come out. But nothing stirred. Only the mosquitoes buzzed and something small rustled in the stubble and scampered away. Then she saw that a small white dog was lying curled up, asleep, at the foot of the caravan step. She moved nearer. The dog lifted its head suddenly, saw her, and came bounding up, wagging its short, stumpy tail. She bent down to stroke it and was greeted with effusive scrabblings and lickings. She sat down on the ground, and the dog, quivering with excitement, alternately snuggled up to her, then ran back to the caravan as if expecting her to follow. Keeping a cautious eye on the open door, Charley did so. Still no one came out.

She sat on the step with the dog beside her, and from there could see inside the caravan. It was empty. The bunk bed was made up and covered with a dark blanket. On the small folding table were a mug, a plate, and a teapot. Someone must be living here. She got up and walked away a little, but the dog followed her, looking up at her expectantly. She played with him, throwing sticks and running after them, then lay, panting, on the ground while he snuffled around her, trying to lick her face.

She talked to him softly, as pleased with his company as he evidently was with hers. "What's your name? My name's Rowan. That's a pretty name, isn't it? It's the name of a tree. Stop pulling my hair,

there's a good chap. Are you lost? I am. Who do you belong to? Are they coming back?"

The dog scrabbled at her impatiently, demanding that she get up and play with him again. At last, when even he seemed to be tiring, she said, "I must go now, but I'll come back tomorrow. Be a good chap and lie down."

She started to move away, but he came trotting after her. Then she saw that a long piece of rope, tied to a hook behind the caravan door, was trailing in the grass. Attached to the end of it was his collar. He must have slipped it. She put it back around his neck, tightening it a notch, and he sat down obediently and watched her move gradually away, as if quite used to this procedure. Whoever he belonged to must care for him, she thought. He was well fed, his coat was sleek, and there was water in his drinking bowl by the door. She wondered who the caravan belonged to. Tomorrow she might find out from Ned.

Much later on, when the fields were turning purple against the orange sky of sunset, Charley ran across to the copse. Only for a minute, she told herself—just to round off this long, golden day.

The blue of twilight was already misting over the birch trees, and the mossy path was like a dark velvet ribbon winding away down to the clearing. She sat in her favorite place under the rowan tree, watching the light gradually fade, and hearing the same whispering, swishing sound in the leaves overhead and the slight rustlings of tiny creatures in the grass. And then—quite suddenly—she heard the long, thin, drawn-out note of some wind instrument, starting from nothing, gradually swelling, then changing to a flight of little notes running downhill, then up again, like footsteps.

It was the same music, and this time her eyes were wide open, so she was not dreaming it! She listened, sitting absolutely still, trying to memorize the phrase that repeated itself over and over, winding its way in and out of the music. It had an unearthly, solitary sweetness, unlike any tune Charley had ever heard, and when it finally died away into silence, she drew a long, deep, shivering breath of pure pleasure. She must remember it. It was music for a fawn to dance to . . .

She sat up, rubbing her eyes. It was late. The moon was coming up, and there was a ground mist rising over the field. She held the tune in her head all the way back, fearful of losing it, trying to hum it under her breath. She made up her bed, put on her pajamas, jeans, and jersey, and lay down under her duffel coat, and still the music was clear in her head.

The moon came up full, like a round white plate in the lilac-colored sky. Behind the copse the setting sun had left an afterglow of crimson. And that night, under the chestnut tree, Charley slept an enchanted sleep.

13

"Who Lives in the Caravan?"

It was dreamlike in the copse early in the morning. Charley awoke with the music of the night before still running in her head, and went straight back there, without even waiting for breakfast. She pushed her way through the bracken, which showered her with dew, ducking low to avoid breaking the huge spiders' webs which were now strung across the path from tree to tree. It was like walking into a picture.

Under the rowan tree she sat, hugging her knees, and stared into an enormous, silvery spider's web which hung, still unbroken, in front of her. Her eyes followed the intricate pattern of the threads—across, along, around, across, along, and around—until everything else became blurred, and she saw only the spider's web, like a delicate net curtain hung in front of a stage. She stared, and then the curtain disappeared, and she saw through to the scene beyond . . .

A beautiful girl—a princess—was walking between the silver birches, leading a fawn by a blue ribbon tied around its neck. The early-morning sunlight flickered down through the leaves, shining first on the princess' long golden hair, then on the fawn's dappled back. In the distance, the turrets of the king's palace rose, golden, into the blue sky, and fountains played on the lawns. The princess was good, and beautiful, and happy, but a shadow lay behind her. A witch had come to live in her father's palace, a witch who, even now, was plotting some evil against the princess. But the fawn was magical. Unknown to the witch, it could lead the princess into an enchanted land where even the most wicked spells would have no power to harm her. The princess and the fawn walked side by side, away down the winding path, appearing and disappearing between the tree trunks, now in sunlight, now in shade, until only an occasional flash of color showed where they were passing; then the trees closed in behind them . . .

A cloud had passed across the sun, and for a moment the copse was in shadow. Then the sun came out full again, the diamond dewdrops on the spider's web quivered and glistened, and Charley blinked. She got up and stretched out her arms. It was going to be another lovely day. She was hungry. And it must be nearly time to go down to Ned's garden.

"How're you going on, all right?" Ned greeted her in his usual way, following it up as he always did with, "All right, eh? That's good, that is."

It was good. Charley watched him pulling up lettuces and thought that in some strange way it had never been so good before. Perhaps because she had woken still remembering the music. Perhaps because it had been so lovely in the copse. Perhaps because . . . She remembered the little white dog who had been so pleased to see her the day before. Now she asked Ned. "Who lives in the caravan, the other side of the little wood?"

Ned scratched his head. "Nobody don't live there," he said.

"But it must belong to somebody?"

"Why, to Mr. Bartlett, surely." And who was Mr. Bartlett, Charley asked. "Why, you should know Mr. Bartlett!" said Ned, looking up at her in some surprise. "Farmer, he is. Lives up your way. All them fields around yours belong to him."

Charley fingered the strips of orange plastic hanging from a string stretched across the garden. "Why do you use these? Why don't you have a proper scarecrow?"

Ned grunted. "These is better. Them old mawkins is old-fashioned. I don't use them no more."

"There's one up near Thornley," said Charley.

"Oh, ay," said Ned, not interested.

"I suppose it belongs to Mr. Bartlett—"

"Ay."

"Like the caravan. Doesn't anybody really live in it?"

"No, nobody don't," said Ned. "Mr. Bartlett's family and their friends uses it sometimes, for holidays and suchlike." He got up, his arms full of lettuces, and looked down at her, grinning. "And that's where I'll be, come Monday," he said.

"What—in the caravan?"

He laughed. "Lor' no! On me holidays, I meant. But you won't find me in no carryvan. It's up at me own place, I'll be, with me feet up."

Charley was dismayed.

"Will you miss me?" he asked, teasing her because she looked so suddenly downcast.

She nodded. She would miss him more than he knew. She wondered about her water. "Won't anyone be here?" she asked.

"Only young Barry," said Ned. "You'd better stop up at your house next week too. Young Barry ain't much company. He'd feel a proper charley with a lassie following him around the garden."

Charley blushed.

"Not but what you ain't been a real help to me," said Ned quickly. "And I means that. Time we was getting on now. It's lettuces today for them-down-there. Rabbit food, that's what that is." He spat on the path. "Why not have the broad beans? I says to 'em. They're nice and hearty now, ready to bust out of the pod. But oh no, she says, we like 'em small, Ned, you knows that." He sighed. "It's the same every year. They must have 'em small—tiddly little things. You don't never want to pick 'em like that, I says. That's a waste of good nature, that is. But d'you think they'll listen to me?" He growled softly at the lettuces. "Filling their bellies with rubbish, that's what it is. They'd do better to buy their veges froze and be done with it." He selected a lettuce from the basket and held it up for Charley to see. "Ain't that a beauty now? I don't know nobody could grow a finer one than that!"

Charley went back to her camp with some of the brightness of the early morning lost. She would miss Ned. Crawling through the hedge into his garden that morning had felt almost like coming home. But she would be all right for water. She had only to get up earlier and fetch it before young Barry came.

The little white dog was still at the caravan, and greeted her with delight when she arrived, prancing about on the end of his rope. Again the caravan was empty, but an upturned wooden box lay outside, with a mug beside it with dregs of tea in the bottom, as if someone had sat out there quite recently. Charley fondled the dog, thought for a moment, then risked it and untied the rope to let him run free.

They chased each other to and fro across the stubble, laughing and barking. He was tugging at a stick she held when he backed suddenly into his water bowl and upset it. She looked around anxiously. Dare she go into the caravan? She walked around to the back and there, to her relief, found a filled water cask standing in the shade, also a small wooden safe with a box of dog biscuits standing on top.

She filled the dog's bowl again, slopping a good deal over because the cask was so heavy. Then, while the dog lapped greedily—as if this were quite different water—she wrote a note on the back of her shopping list. *"Your dog's water got upset so I filled it"*—this in case the lower level of water in the cask should be noticed. She paused, wondering whether to sign it, decided not, and added, *"He slipped his collar yesterday, so I tightened it."* That would show she was not only well intentioned but responsible as well.

She left the note on the box, under the mug, and before she left, she tied the dog up again.

Back in her camp, looking for something to eat, it dawned on her suddenly that it was Friday. That would be the *fourth* day she had been away—not the third, as she had been thinking. And she had reckoned that on the fourth day everyone would know she was lost, and be looking for her! What food had she left? There was one orange, a small hunk of stale bread, and the remaining chocolates, now melted into a soft, sticky mass—at least it would be a relief not to have to ration them out, two at a time anymore. She must buy more food today. The fruitcake (sent by Aunt Emm for Auntie Louie) did not count. She had forgotten to collect windfalls that morning, and those she had left were mostly rotten.

The dairy in Brinchester was too near home now. If she was being searched for, she would probably be recognized and questioned, no matter how much she pretended to be dumb. There was only one thing for it; she must walk into Frickham. It was farther away, but it was a bigger place, and a solitary, scruffy girl would be less noticeable there.

14

Police!

So now they all knew she was lost!

What were they thinking? Aunt Emm would be furious, and serve her right, serve her right, serve her right, Charley thought, walking in time to the words. But she could not any longer keep up the same anger she had once had. The rage had gone out of it. She had gloated too often over the idea of Aunt Emm's face when she heard Charley had run away. It was like an old story now—one she had grown tired of. It had nothing to do with this hazy, dreamy afternoon, and the long walk between the overgrown, dusty hedges.

And when she thought of Auntie Louie, she found it difficult, even, not to feel a little sorry for her. She knew just how she would look, her blue eyes already magnified by the thick lenses of her glasses, looking larger than ever now they were filled with alarm. She would be trying to get busy about finding Charley, but without the least idea how to set about it, and every now and then she would be saying, "There now, and it's all my fault for saying I didn't want the poor lamb!" Charley imagined her adding that of course she wanted her—had wanted her all along. She had only said she didn't because—because—because what?

Here Charley's mind went blank. She could not imagine anything that would have made Auntie Louie say so flatly that she didn't want her. Over and over again she had looked at that strip of paper, feeling sure she must have misread it somehow. But always it had said the same unmistakable thing—*I don't want Charley. You know that . . .*

She was jerked suddenly out of her thoughts. Around a bend in the road a policeman had appeared, riding steadily toward her on a bicycle. She leapt backward into the hedge, pressing herself as far back as she could into the prickly branches. There was no time to run away. It was too late to hide. She stared, like a hypnotized rabbit, as man and bicycle grew larger and larger, drawing nearer every moment. What should she say? Who could she pretend to be?

Then, when she could even hear the faint ticking

of the bicycle wheels, something like a small miracle occurred. There was a sudden explosive sound from beyond the hedge opposite. A motor was being started up in the field. It popped, spluttered, fell silent, then started up again. The policeman turned his head automatically, and kept it turned, still pedaling slowly along and watching through the gaps in the hedge as a tractor began moving away across the field. A moment later, and he had passed her!

All clear—as long as he didn't look back. And he didn't. She waited until he was out of sight, then walked quickly on. What a stroke of luck that had been! And what another stroke of luck that she should be walking away from Market Barnham just as he was going in!

So she was right. The search had begun. He would go first to Auntie Louie's, she supposed. What if she had still been in hen house corner and he had come crashing through the hedge at the bottom of the garden! How silly it would have looked to be found camping within a stone's throw of the house! She thought with satisfaction of the careful way she had hidden all her things. Unless he actually went around and looked inside the hen house, he would never know she had been there. (Poor man, might he miss promotion for having let her slip through his fingers so easily?)

A long straight road stretched ahead of her. She hurried on. Fields, haystacks, and the odd farm building were left behind, but the distant roofs seemed to get no nearer. A square red-brick house stood alone. "I'll stop for a rest when I get there," she said to herself. "Perhaps someone will offer me a cup of tea when they see how incredibly hot and thirsty I am." How did one look incredibly hot and thirsty? She thrust her head forward, let her mouth hang open, and shuffled along, occasionally passing a weary hand over her forehead. But it wouldn't do. She was pretty sure she only looked incredibly foolish. She must rely on their common sense and kindness of heart. But when she reached the house, glancing hopefully sideways at the windows and only limping a little, she was startled to see a cement plaque over the door with the words "Norfolk County Constabulary" carved on it in large letters. Who would have thought such an ordinary-looking house could be a police station?

She walked jauntily past (looking not in the *least* tired), then ran without stopping all the way through the next village and out the other side. That had been a near thing!

It was only when she came into Frickham, and saw how many people and cars there were, that she realized she had been silly. Because it was a bigger place, there would be more police. And they would have been notified by now, and be on the lookout for her. But it was too late to go back.

She darted into the first grocer's she came to—a self-service store—and bought a tin of luncheon meat, a loaf, and some more cheese. There were a number of people in the shop, but she avoided looking at any of them and was relieved when no one tapped her on the shoulder. The woman at the pay desk barely glanced at her, and a moment later she was out in the narrow, crowded street again.

The air was close and heavy with the smell of fish-and-chips, petrol, and people. An hour ago she would have been glad of the fish-and-chips, but now she was not hungry. She wanted an ice-cream. Glancing quickly to left and right, she scurried down to the kiosk in the marketplace and treated herself to a double ice-cream cone. If she was going to be caught, she would at least have that first. But she was not going to be caught—if she could help it.

She licked hurriedly, with sidelong glances, hiding as well as she could between two stalls. "Out of me way, now!" said a woman bustling past. "Don't stand in gangway, lass. What are you doing here, any road?" she added with sudden suspicion. Charley, realizing the woman thought she was there to steal something, moved out again into the open.

A chemist's shop caught her eye. She remembered

the soap, and was halfway over the road when she was held up by a stream of passing cars. She glanced around and saw to her horror that a policeman was standing only a few feet away from her, directing the traffic. In sudden panic, she lunged as if to cross. There was a shout behind her, and she felt herself pulled sharply back.

"Eh, but that's dangerous, that is!" said a stout man in leather leggings. "Ain't you never learned your highway code?" He held her in a firm grip until the traffic stopped and they were allowed to cross. Then, with her head down, Charley bolted across the road, past the chemist's, and down a side turning. She was out of breath by the time she allowed herself to look back. No one was following her. More slowly now, she sauntered past a shoe mender's, a café, a picture frame maker's. The next shop had a case of stuffed birds in the window. Another, a pile of mattresses. In none did it seem likely they would sell soap. Not noticing the direction she took, she was dismayed at last to find herself back in the market-place, not fifty yards from the chemist's.

A man in a felt hat was standing on the opposite pavement. He appeared to recognize her, and started across the road. She froze. Obviously he was going to speak to her. Suffering codfish, a plainclothesman? Her feet seemed fixed to the ground as he came towards her hesitantly.

"I—er—I'm looking for—" he gave her an apologetic smile. Charley tried to smile back, but her mouth felt stiff and peculiar. "Looking for—"

"Yes?" Charley felt her eyes actually crossing as she did her utmost to look interested and helpful.

"The—er—I think it's called El Serrano. I think it may be a coffee bar. I promised to meet my young lady there, but I'm a stranger in these parts—"

Charley was so relieved she could not even speak. She shrugged and shook her head, and he moved away to ask someone else. After this she was ready to run if anyone so much as looked at her. It was a relief to reach the chemist's, slip inside, and buy a cake of soap.

When she came out, the policeman was still there, directing the traffic. If he had recognized her he seemed quite unconcerned now. So did everyone else. People passed up and down the pavement, went into shops, crossed over the road, but none of them showed any particular interest in her. She was safer, perhaps, than she had thought. She stood with her back to the shopwindow, and stared at the policeman, daring him to see her. It seemed only fair to give him the chance now. He would be sure to have her description. Aunt Emm might even have sent the police a photograph. (Time enough to run when he recognized her. Even then he could hardly leave the traffic to chase after her.) But nothing happened.

Once, during a lull, he glanced straight across at her and she jumped, but for all the interest he showed, she might have been any other girl come into town to look at the shops.

She was surprised. She moved forward to the curb and walked up and down, deliberately keeping in full view of him. But still nothing happened. She retreated again to the shopwindow and leaned up against it, staring out into the road. And gradually she allowed herself to realize the truth. She was not being searched for at all. Life in Frickham was going on no differently from the way it always did.

Probably it was the same at home, too—except that they would all be busy packing and thinking about their own holidays now. They were not bothering to search for her, knowing she would turn up as she always did, when she felt like it. (But she'd never run away for more than a few hours before! Surely they remembered that?) Weren't they worried in case she was hungry or lonely? Auntie Louie *must* have let them know she had never arrived . . .

No, if she was uncomfortable or lonely, it was her own fault. That would be her punishment, brought on by no one but herself. She could almost hear Aunt Emm saying it.

A group of children came along with their mother and stopped outside the chemist's. They jostled each other at the window, pointing things out, chattering eagerly, suggesting, arguing. They were obviously choosing a present for someone. Charley looked at them with scorn, hating them for their clean, bright clothes and well brushed hair. Soppy kids. Fancy shopping all in a gaggle like that with your mother. She, at least, was independent.

The woman turned and caught her lowering glare. "I'm sorry!" she said with a quick smile. "Are we crowding you out? Here, children, move up!"

But Charley turned her back on them and walked away. She would have much preferred it if the woman had been rude to her. She turned back down the side street, and went into the café for a fizzy drink. She needed somewhere to think.

Wasn't anyone missing her? Not even Toby? No, Toby would be glad she wasn't there to bully him. What about Giles, then? Mightn't he be sorry now and wish he hadn't jeered at her quite so much? After all, it was he who had suggested she run away and make a proper job of it in the first place. Come to think of it, he might—secretly—be feeling quite worried about her, even a little guilty. But of course he wouldn't dare tell Aunt Emm. Poor Giles. Perhaps she would be kind and send him a postcard, just so he should know she was all right. She began to build up a new picture of Giles in her mind. A picture of a kind and loving elder brother who only treated her harshly because he wanted her to learn to look after herself—the same as he did. Yes, he was probably worried sick about her by now. He would never show it, but then he never showed his affection for her either. That didn't mean anything.

She paid for her drink and hurried out into the street again. She would buy a postcard now, before the shops shut. The sky seemed to be darkening already. Filled with gratitude to the new, imaginary Giles, she bought a picture postcard of the marketplace, and in the post office wrote on the back of it, *"Dear Giles, I am quite all right so you needn't worry about me at all. Tell Toby I've got some nougat to make up for the toffee bar, but it's in the secret place where I'm living. Love from Charley."*

That should make him feel better, she thought as she posted it outside. It would remind them of her, too.

The post office clock said only a quarter to five after all, so there was no question of the shops shutting yet. She bought three bananas and an iced bun on her way back to the marketplace, and as she passed the chemist's, she stopped for a moment to look in the window, curious to see what that family of children had found so much to argue about.

There were all the usual things there—hot-water bottles, boxes of different kinds of soap, and jars of colored bath salts. And toward the front of the window were large pale-pink and blue powder puffs, and lavender sachets decorated with loops and bows of ribbon, and trimmed with lace. Ladies' rubbish, Giles would have called them. Useless, and a waste of money, Aunt Emm would have said. And yet they were pretty . . .

She wondered what the family had chosen for their present. What would she herself have chosen, if she had known the right sort of person to buy it for—the sort of person who liked things like that? Suppose, even, that Charley herself were going to be given one for a present, which would she choose?

She made up her mind, and on a sudden impulse, opened the shop door and went in.

15

Nightmare

The walk back seemed strange. Everything was different now. They knew she had run away, and were not worried or alarmed, but merely waiting until she had had enough of it and decided to turn up at Holmdene. The realization made Charley feel oddly at a loose end. What happened next? She was surprised, and a little flattered, that Aunt Emm thought she was old enough and responsible enough to look after herself, but she was also disappointed.

The weather had changed, too. The countryside looked different. The fields of stubble, usually golden in the early-evening sunlight, were dead and colorless. A blight seemed to have come over everything.

She met scarcely anyone. Once a boy passed on a bicycle with a transistor hanging from the handlebars, and the sudden burst of pop music, fading a few seconds later, made the road seem longer and emptier than ever. The sun, which had disappeared since early afternoon, was now setting in streaks of lurid yellow, and the air was so close and heavy that Charley fancied she still had the oily smell of fish-and-chips and petrol in her nostrils. She trudged on, bathed in a clammy sweat.

About halfway back, a truck overtook her and drew up alongside, and a man leaned out of the driving cab.

"Want a lift, lassie? How far you going?"

Charley shook her head automatically. She knew that lifts must never be accepted from strangers, no matter how tempting, but as he looked kind—even concerned—she added, "I like walking, but thank you very much."

He looked at her doubtfully. "I was thinking you looked as if you'd walked far enough," he said. "You ain't lost, are you?"

"Oh, no!" Charley looked surprised. "No—I live over there"—she waved a hand vaguely—"quite near."

He nodded, smiled, and drove away, and she walked on into the streaky yellow sunset.

Dusk came earlier that night, and with it an ominous smell of burning. Back in hen house corner, Charley sniffed the air and looked around. The sky was heavily overcast, but just beyond the copse, in the direction of Brinchester, a heavy cloud hung in the still air, looking suspiciously like smoke. She was filled with uneasiness. Could the caravan be on fire? There were no houses near. Ought she to go and see? It would soon be dark. But what about the little dog? Suppose he was still alone?

She began running across the field with some vague idea of rescuing him and bringing him back

with her, thinking, even as she stumbled through the rough grass, that she would be particularly glad of his company tonight. But as she neared the top of the field she heard movements, voices, and two dark figures appeared from around the outer edge of the copse.

She flopped down in the grass and lay flat on her

stomach, scarcely breathing as they crossed the field ahead of her and disappeared into the darkness. But for a moment she had seen, silhouetted against the sky, the shapes of two men with a small dog trotting along beside them. And one of the men had been carrying a gun!

She got up shakily. What were they going to do? Why were they taking the dog away? The smell of burning was stronger here and there was a flickering light in the sky beyond the trees. There *was* a fire, and they must have seen it. But why the gun? She ran, panting, back to her camp, her mind filled with unreasoning fears. Perhaps they were going to shoot the dog. The caravan was burned to the ground, and they had nowhere to keep him. Perhaps they were tramps, anyway, and had no right to have been there.

Trembling, she unpacked the food she had bought. She must keep her mind on other things. Tomorrow she would find out what had happened. For the moment she must be as sensible as Aunt Emm evidently thought she was. It was too late now to go over to the copse, too dark to open a tin, even; but she ate some cheese and bread, and gradually the trembling ceased. Perhaps it had been partly hunger. She had not eaten properly all day and had not realized before how empty she was.

Her limbs ached with tiredness. As she got ready for bed, she knew she would be asleep almost as soon as she closed her eyes. Beyond the copse she could still see the faint, flickering glow in the sky, and as she lay down she heard, in the far distance, the sound of a shot. But she was too tired to be frightened anymore. She turned over and sank immediately into a heavy sleep.

Charley was having a terrible dream. She was coming home from school much later than usual. It was quite dark. When she knocked on the front door of her home, a completely strange woman opened it and asked her what she wanted. Charley apologized and said she had made a mistake. She was beginning to feel frightened but trying not to show it. Then, as she walked away, she remembered that of course they didn't live in that house anymore. It was the one they had lived in when she was very small.

Next, in her dream, she found herself knocking at the door of the house they lived in now, but here the same thing happened. Someone quite strange opened the door and said, "Oh, no, your parents have gone away! Don't you remember?"

Charley went away again, feeling foolish and with the fear mounting inside her. Then she thought of Auntie Louie. She would go there, but she must hurry. It was late, and before long they would have gone to bed. She was trying to hurry up Bell Lane—only it looked quite different—her legs were like lead

133

and she hardly seemed to be moving, and there was a rushing noise in the air all around her. She stumbled in at the gate and up to the front door, and began banging on it with her bare fists, but they made no sound. She shouted, "Auntie Louie!" at the top of her voice—and woke to hear the remains of the little squawk she had actually made still sounding in her ears. The rushing noise in the air was real, though. It was heavy rain falling on the leaves overhead and pattering down through the branches.

She sprang up in terror, uncertain for a moment where she was, then remembered with relief that Auntie Louie was still near at hand. She must get to her quickly. At once. Now. Her nightmare still hung about her and she plunged blindly along by the hedge, feeling as if she were being pursued. But she had missed the opening in the hedge. She scrabbled in the branches, tearing her hands on thorns, and realized she must be several gardens along already. She dared not stop. She plunged on, past the ends of the gardens, through the gap at the bottom, and out into Bell Lane. She would have to run all the way up again, but it was better than staying in that terrible, nightmarish corner under the chestnut tree. She remembered the flickering light in the sky, and the distant shot she had heard just before falling asleep, but pushed the memory back quickly. She must not think . . . must not remember anything . . . just keep running . . . without stopping. Only when she got to Auntie Louie's would she be safe.

Her breath came in deep, tearing gasps and her saliva seemed to have turned to glue in her mouth. Her legs grew heavier with every step until they felt like lead, and she scarcely seemed to be moving. It was her nightmare over again, but this time it was real. She was living it. When at last she reached the top of the lane and pushed open the gate of Holmdene, she almost fell into the garden.

She tottered the few steps to the front door and, with no breath left to shout, gasped, "Auntie Louie, Auntie Louie!" and beat her hands frenziedly on the door. Then she found the bell push. She put her finger on it, and kept it there while she leaned, panting, against the doorpost.

No one came. She tried to remember what Aunt Emm had said—that they were going to Hunstanton in early October. Surely it couldn't be October already? That would be nearly a month ahead, and she had only been away about a week. How many nights? She began counting desperately. The night in the garden—that strange first night. The night in the field, after she'd fallen asleep in the copse. The next night in the field, after she'd heard the music again. And the night when there was a fire—but that had been only last night—no, tonight. That only made four.

The rain had stopped suddenly. She could hear water running down the side of the road and gurgling into a drain, but no sound came from inside the house. No footsteps running, no startled exclamations, no fumbling with the bolts. She pushed the flap of the letter box and called into the blackness, "Auntie Louie, let me in! It's me—Charley. Let me in!" Then she put her ear to the opening. No sound at all from inside. No one there. And from outside, only the sound of her own heavy breathing, and the drip, drip, drip of the rain overflowing from the gutter and falling on the concrete path. Auntie Louie must have gone away.

She sank down on the doorstep and burst into tears.

16

No More Milk, Thank You

Damp, stiff, and covered with dirt and cobwebs, Charley crept out of the Hewitts' tool shed in the early morning, and crawled back through the hedge.

The field was sodden after last night's rain, and there was a hot steaminess everywhere. It was as though the world had sunk under water during the night and now everything was muffled. Her duffel coat and mackintosh were soaked, and the ground under the tree was a muddy swamp. Hen house corner looked a cheerless, desolate place and the flavor of her nightmare still seemed to hang about the place. She felt dazed and not quite real.

Could it be true that Auntie Louie had gone away? No, she did not believe that now. It had all been part of her nightmare. Probably she had not made half as much noise as she had imagined. She ate her breakfast of a banana and the remains of the chocolates sitting on the upturned bucket and thinking how lucky it was that no one had heard her. What an idiot she would have looked if they'd woken up and found her squawking and gibbering on the doorstep in the middle of the night! It was one thing to be a fool on purpose, but to be a fool by mistake . . .

Nevertheless, she must make sure. She must go around to Holmdene again. If Auntie Louie was there and happened to see her, well—then she could invite Charley in if she wanted. She would not go specially out of her way to be seen, but she must know for certain that they were still there. She would go around by the road. It would look better than just turning up from the back garden. She remembered the fruitcake. That would make a good excuse for going.

The mist was curling away and the sun beginning to break through the haze as Charley set off for Holmdene. She walked slowly, casually, reminding herself that she was not going for a visit—only to make sure they were there. But if they *should* ask her in . . .

As she neared the turning up to Bell Lane, she saw a man approaching from the opposite direction. It was the clergyman she had met that first afternoon. She stopped, remembered, then limped quickly on, and up the lane. But before she had gone more than a few yards, he had caught her up. He stopped and smiled. "Hallo," he said.

"Hallo," said Charley.

He hesitated, his eyes flicking over her quickly, then nodded at the parcel she was carrying.

"Is that heavy? I mean I can carry it for you if you like. You're looking rather done up, and I'd quite like to walk up that way again. You're staying in Bell Lane, aren't you? I believe that's where I saw you before."

Charley evaded the question and answered his last remark. "Yes, you were coming down. I saw you, too. But it's all right, thank you. It's not heavy. It's. a cake."

"Oh. Oh, I see. In that case it ought to be very light, oughtn't it?" He laughed at his little joke, but anxiously, as if his mind were really on something else. Charley had felt him noticing her untidiness. Now she felt him carefully not noticing it. She glanced down at herself. Her skirt was very torn and she was dreadfully dirty.

"Those are some nasty bruises you've got," he said, his eyes following hers. "On your legs. How did that happen?"

She shrugged. "I don't remember. I must go," she added hurriedly, but trying to sound apologetic at the same time.

"Yes—yes, of course. I expect someone's waiting for

you with that cake, aren't they?" He looked earnestly into her eyes for a moment as if hoping for a reply, then, as she was silent, hurried on, "I was just thinking—just wondering—perhaps you'd like to come to our Sunday school? It's at half past two in the church hall. Tomorrow. It would be nice if you would. I could tell Miss Joyce to look out for you. Tell me your name!" He saw the sudden alarm in her eyes. "No, no need to worry. There's no compulsion, you know! I only meant it would be nice if you would. We'd be glad to see you. Well, I must be hurrying along. Good-bye."

He started to move away, then turned back. "And no need to worry about what to wear or anything," he said, deliberately keeping his eyes away from her clothes and looking searchingly into her face. "You could come as you are. Perhaps wash your hands, that's all." He smiled, and hurried away down the road.

Charley waited until he was out of sight, then went on up Bell Lane. He was a nice man. She wondered why he had looked so worried. Perhaps he didn't have enough children coming to his Sunday school, and he had to stop strangers in the road to invite them.

Holmdene had its usual blind face on. Charley went around the side of the house and stood, listening, within a few feet of the scullery window. From

here she should be able to hear their voices, or at least the radio. But all was silent. No smell of frying bacon either. She wondered what the time was.

She went on around. The back door was shut; so was the scullery window. After a moment she tried the door, tentatively, thinking she might at least put the cake down inside. But it was locked. She felt for the key over the lintel. It was not there. She went to the window and stood on tiptoe, looking in. The draining board was empty. There was no sign of breakfast things. Not even a teapot. She stepped back. A piece of crumpled paper lay at her feet, still limp with rain. She picked it up and read *"No more milk, thank you."*

So it was true! They had gone away!

For a moment she could hardly believe it. She was astonished, furious, hurt, outraged. To go away when they knew she might be turning up at any moment! How could Auntie Louie have done such a thing? Even if she didn't want her? Even if her husband didn't like children?

What was she to do now? Should she camp here in the garden, or would it be even worse, knowing the house was empty behind her? She heard the sound of a door opening, followed by shuffling footsteps and the clang of a dustbin lid next door. That would be old Mrs. Wilks going out to empty her ashes. She was deaf and arthritic and rarely went out of doors, but her sharp eyes were beady and suspicious. Charley remembered her as an unfriendly, ill-tempered old woman who had snarled at her over the fence last summer and refused to return the ball she had thrown over by mistake. Auntie Louie had said not to worry, she was like that with everyone. Mrs. Wilks would be worse than useless now. Where, then, would Charley feel safe? Ned's garden—if only he wasn't going away. But there would be no one there at night.

She stood holding her breath until the shuffling footsteps had returned and the door closed again, then she took hold of the back door handle and rattled it hard. There was no give in the door. The bolts must have been pulled across inside.

She shouted silently, furiously, at the closed door. "I hate you! I hope you both get drowned and run over, and have a perfectly beastly holiday!" Then she went down the garden and crawled back into hen house corner.

More than ever now it had become a desolate, lonely place. Not for anything would she spend another night there now she knew the Hewitts had gone. She must get away. But where to?

She stood irresolutely under the dripping chestnut tree while the wood pigeon burbled in the distance, "Oh you poor *thing*, Charley! Oh you poor *thing*, Charley!"—on and on. Stupid thing. *Stupid* thing! If she had a gun, she would shoot it. No silly bird could make her cry. She opened her mouth wide and bit at the empty air, beating her clenched fists against her sides. Then with trembling hands she began collecting her things together.

17

In the Copse

She must get away. Quickly. She stacked her be-
longings in a pile behind the hen house, ready to be
moved as soon as she knew where, and went across
the field to look for a likely place. The copse seemed
the obvious choice, but it would be so lonely at
nights . . . She remembered the caravan. Had it really
been burned down? She hurried around the outer
edge of the trees.

There was still an acrid smell of burning in the
heavy air. She turned the corner and saw that the
field was now patterned with charred black stripes
running from end to end. So that was it! They had
been burning the stubble . . . She ran on a few steps,
then stopped suddenly. In the distance, opposite to
where the caravan stood, a boy was moving about

with a small white dog at his heels. Relieved, she stepped back into the trees.

So the caravan had not been burned down. And tramps were not living in it. As far as she had been able to tell from that distance, the boy was a little taller than Giles, and had been wearing khaki shorts. And the dog was all right. She felt happier now.

The caravan could be her new "home." A pretend one only, but she could camp near it. It would not matter that no one knew she was there, so long as she knew they were. She pushed her way through brambles and nettles farther into the copse, keeping in the general direction of the caravan, and came out on a gentle slope covered with bushes, bracken, and silver birches. A little way farther, and she saw the corner of the caravan roof jutting out from under the bank below her. Just what she had hoped to see!

A few yards back up the slope she chose a reasonably level place between bushes and began clearing it, pulling up nettles and trampling down the bracken. This should be her new camping place. The bracken would make a good mattress.

It took a long time to bring all her things across the field, and by the time she had even dragged her "table" and "chair" across, the sun was blazing in the purplish-blue sky and it was hotter than ever. Her arms and legs were stinging with sunburn and nettle stings, and the mosquitoes were a plague. She was

glad to get back to the garden tap at Holmdene and
duck her head under the water. Afterward she filled
her bucket and stood for a moment, thinking. She
would like the Hewitts to know she had been there.
She pulled a stump of pencil from her pocket and
wrote, bitterly, on the back of the note left out for
the milkman, *"Thank you for not having me,"* and
left it on the step under a stone. Then she turned her
back on Holmdene.

The important thing now was to make her new
camp feel like home before nightfall. And the only
way to make a place feel like home was to live in it.
She spread out her mackintosh on the bracken and
lay down on it to get used to the new view. Then she
laid the box table with her plate and mug, and filled
the potted meat jar with a sprig of purple mallow,
one or two dog daisies, and some poppies she had
picked in the field. She found blackberries in the
bushes and heaped some on the plate. That seemed
right—like washing her face in dew—and she wished
she could find more things to eat just growing naturally, the way people did in stories. Somehow the
cheese, sweating in its greaseproof paper, looked all
wrong. She missed having the hen house as a cupboard. Her painting things would have to go in the
suitcase now, and this she slid under a bush, out of
sight, along with her shoes and various other things.

It was a strange, long day. She remembered Ned,

whom she had not seen since yesterday, and who would be going on holiday tomorrow, and ran down to the garden. But he had gone. Surprised, she went down as far as the greenhouse and found the door padlocked. But it was still bright sunlight! It could not be evening already. Then she remembered it was Saturday. He had gone at midday, and she had not said good-bye to him!

Now, more than ever, everything seemed to have changed. Everyone she knew had gone—with the exception of the dog, and she dared not visit him in case the strange boy was still there. She felt lost. She was lost. She hurried back to her new camp. If she was lost, she must not look like it. She must tidy herself up, make herself look as if she belonged somewhere. She got out her hairbrush and began brushing her hair feverishly.

Then she remembered the clergyman. He was one person she knew in Market Barnham anyway. "Perhaps you would like to come to our Sunday school," he had said. It had been almost like an invitation. "I'll tell Miss Joyce to look out for you," (whoever Miss Joyce was). Should she go? Why not? He had obviously been needing more people, and she had never been to Sunday school before . . . She went to get her clothes out, then changed her mind. It might rain again tonight. Better wait till tomorrow, then decide what to wear.

But she went back to Holmdene with her new cake
of soap and washed her face, hands and knees under
the running garden tap. The place gave her the
creeps now. It was dank and smelled of cabbage stalks
and drains. There were snails stuck to the fence
above the tap, and an enormous, fleshy pink worm
slithered over the brick on which she had balanced
her soap. She skidded on a slug as she ran back down
the path and shuddered with sudden horror.

It was a relief to get away again.

Charley sat under the rowan tree. It seemed ages
since this morning when she had stood in the Hewitts' garden, looking at that note for the milkman
and trying to grasp the fact that they had gone away.
Now it did not matter at all. It was as if it had
happened to someone else, a long time ago—someone
with the ridiculous name of Charley, who was neither a boy nor a proper girl, but a sort of fool-on-
purpose, someone about whom people wrote, *I don't
want Charley. You know that . . .*

But she—she was Rowan, the beautiful princess,
who lived in this forest with a fawn as her only
companion. A vile old witch had turned her out of
her kingdom. She had appeared one day, as ugly as
an old boot, with a small mustache and a creased,
yellow face, and she had hated Rowan—because she
herself was ugly and no one liked her—and she had

149

turned her out of the palace while the king was away in a foreign land.

She had smiled, with a horrible false smile, and told the princess she was being sent away on a holiday. But in reality she was being sent to a place where no one lived—where no one had lived for years and years—where slugs and snails and wood lice grown as big as toads, crawled over the slimy ground and gurgled in the drains. The witch had sent her away, hoping she would die in solitude.

The princess wandered into the forest and sat down under a rowan tree and wept, and her tears watered her hair until at last it grew so long that it wound itself around and around the tree roots. She cried out in despair, "Alas, I shall die here, and the crows will peck out my eyes, and my bones will whiten in the sun, and no one will ever know!"

Then the Princess Rowan remembered a magic tune she had once learned. It was still in the back of her mind, but she could not remember it clearly enough to sing it out loud. And yet she knew that if only she could, everything would be all right. She sat there a long while trying to remember it, and then, suddenly, it came back to her and she sang it in a clear, golden voice. And the magic worked! Immediately a beautiful little pale-brown fawn came dancing through the dappled sunlight, lifting its head from side to side to hear where the music came from, and it found her there under the rowan tree. It sat beside her, and gently unwound her hair from the tree roots with its soft mouth.

"Oh, thank you!" she cried, "you have set me free!" and she made a garland of mallow, and poppies, and daisies to hang around the fawn's neck. It was timid at first, afraid she might be going to imprison it, but she knelt very still in the grass until at last it came up quite close and nuzzled against her and allowed her to slip the garland over its head. And now they *lived* together, happily ever after in the forest, on blackberries, and apples, and nuts, and . . . no, not cheese . . .

Charley got up and stretched her legs. She had sat still for so long that they had gone numb. The fawn's music was still wafting through the trees and she would have liked to stay longer, but there was a smell of evening in the air and she must get back to her camp before the sun went down. Later, she knew, it would become a strange, new place, with shadows in unfamiliar corners—lonely, perhaps frightening. Now, with the music still in her ears, she would find her way back and get ready for bed. She would slide straight from this lovely waking dream into real sleep, without allowing herself to wake up and become Charley again.

Dizzy with sleep and sunshine, and the strangeness

of that long, hot day, she wandered back through the copse and around the outer edge of the trees to the track she had made that morning. She drifted through the bracken and brambles, came out onto the slope and saw her bed laid out in a haze of greenness. Even the air was green under the birch trees.

She lay down. The bracken was soft and springy beneath her, and above her the leaves hung like curtains. She was enclosed in greenness, like Titania. She was safe. The caravan was near, so was the dog, and the music was still dropping out of the trees . . .

Rowan fell asleep—Charley was forgotten.

18

To Sunday School in a Green Dress

Charley awoke to hear the wood pigeon, surprisingly close at hand, burbling insistently, "How are you *now*, Charley? How are you *now*, Charley?"

She sat up and felt her scratched and bruised legs gingerly. "Not so good," she said. "How are you?"

"Oh my poor *toe*, Charley! Oh my poor *toe*, Charley!"

"Oh, you poor thing," said Charley, "but there's nothing I can do about it. There's nothing I can do about my own hurts either. I think we're both poor things."

Her head ached and one of the mosquito bites had swollen into an angry red lump on her arm. Then she remembered—Sunday school. Today!

She forgot her aches and pains in turning out her

suitcase. Her shirts were filthy. It looked as if it would have to be the best green dress. But she could not find the belt anywhere—funny, she hadn't worn it since she'd come away—never mind, she must wear it without. The dress was horribly crumpled. It was made of that kind of springy, silky material that, once creased, remains creased and nothing but an iron can set right. But she hung it out hopefully over the branch of a tree. The air might smooth it out.

She pulled her shoes out from under the bush. The caked mud had hardened on them and the uppers had gone a curious green color. Mold had formed on them. But they would have to do. She unrolled a pair of socks. They looked very white and seemed to accentuate the peculiar color of her legs which, as well as being sunburned, were purple and red with bruises and scratches, and streaked with green where she had savagely rubbed them with dock leaves to ease the nettle stings. Better not wear the socks, perhaps. Luckily her legs would be hidden under a desk most of the time. She imagined Sunday school would be much the same as ordinary school, only with different lessons.

There was no way of knowing the exact time. Half past two, he had said. She had grown used to judging time roughly—the smells and sounds of afternoon were quite different from those of morning or evening—but it would be difficult to judge it within half an hour. She decided to get ready early and go down into Market Barnham well beforehand.

Dressed, she looked down at herself doubtfully, at her crumpled dress hanging like a shapeless tent—it looked awful without its belt!—and at her mottled, greenish shoes, and her bare bruised legs. Did she look as if she lived in a house? Hardly. The only thing to do, then, was to look as if it was on purpose. (If only she had a mirror!) Green . . . everything about her was green, her dress, her shoes, even her legs—in patches. Perhaps she could dye them green all over, make them look like stockings? She found more dock leaves, and rubbed until her legs burned. They were certainly greener, but still streaky. She pulled some strings of bryony from the bushes and wound them around her waist to make a belt—that was better—she mustn't overdo it, though. She picked some convolvulus to put in her hair and immediately felt more dressed—almost like a bridesmaid . . . or a wood nymph.

She took a long time dressing.

It smelled like early Sunday afternoon as Charley set off across the fields to Market Barnham. It felt rather like it, too, because she was having to walk carefully—the way she did when she was wearing best clothes and going out to tea—otherwise her belt of twisted bryony was likely to come undone and fall off.

The blackberries were ripe and black on the hedges. She picked them as she went along, enjoying the sight of her brown hand searching among the dark purplish-green leaves. She had never been so brown before. It looked like someone else's hand. Perhaps all of her looked like someone else by now. She felt like someone else, too, she thought, as she sat in the grass to eat the blackberries, and wondered whether even Auntie Louie would recognize her if she saw her now.

And yet, in a way, she hardly felt like a person at all. Sitting there in the dreamy autumn sunshine, she was wrapped around in the same soft, peach-colored haze as the fields and hedges and haystacks; no longer looking at them from outside, but part of them—like the earwig crawling across her leg, and the dry wisps of bladder campion rustling against her elbow. *I shall never be the same again*, she thought. *Even in a school blazer I shall know that I'm really part of a blackberry hedge, first cousin to an earwig . . .*

But she was forgetting about Sunday school! She sprang up, catching her foot in her skirt, and felt something give. A moment later it was flapping against the back of her leg as she walked. The hem was coming undone. Suffering codfish, now what? No needle, no cotton, no pins. She sighed, pulled out the remaining threads, and twirled around to make the dress hang free. It had been a deep hem to allow for growing, now the skirt reached halfway to her ankles. All the better, it would hide her legs. She swayed from side to side. It felt rather good. There was a graceful feeling about having so much skirt. It made you feel like dancing. She twirled again, then took off her shoes and danced all the way down to the road.

There she found she had lost her bryony belt after all and had to go back. It was lying halfway up the field. She retied it, put on her shoes, and hurried down again. But by the time she reached the church hall she was late.

The door was slightly open. Charley put her ear to it and heard a woman's voice talking inside. It sounded as if she were telling a story. She opened the door a little wider and went in. The voice stopped suddenly in mid-sentence and she saw a young woman in a blue suit, staring at her with startled, round blue eyes. She waited quietly just inside the door.

"Yes?" said the young woman. Charley waited. "Yes?" she said again, and Charley, realizing she was being asked something, said, "I'm sorry, I didn't hear the question. I've only just come in."

The young woman, who she supposed must be Miss Joyce, gave a nervous laugh, opened her mouth, shut it again, then pointed to a chair at the end of a row. Charley sat down. Miss Joyce cleared her throat, gave her a frightened glance, and went on

with her story. Charley looked around the room.
   Sunday school was totally different from what she
had expected. There were no desks and no black-
board. The children were sitting in rows facing Miss
Joyce, though at the moment their heads were all

turned in Charley's direction. Miss Joyce—still telling her story—said, "And they were all hungry because they hadn't thought of bringing any food with them turn round children and listen to me," all in one breath. They all turned, except one girl rather older

than the rest, whom Charley recognized as the girl who had been sucking an iced lolly when she met her in the road. She was staring at Charley now as if she didn't quite believe she was real. Charley ignored her, and, fixing her eyes earnestly on Miss Joyce, listened attentively.

The story was about the Feeding of the Five Thousand. When it was over, there was a general scramble toward a table up at the front. Charley looked at Miss Joyce, who seemed to be trying not to see her, then got up and followed the others. It seemed that the children were now going to draw pictures or make models of the story they had heard, and were going up to fetch their materials, but by the time Charley realized this, the pencils and crayons had all gone, and all that was left on the table was a large lump of mud-colored clay.

She stared at it doubtfully. Miss Joyce nodded her head at her, smiled sweetly, said, "That's right, that's right," and looked quickly away again. Charley took it back to her place and used it to make a careful but exaggerated likeness of Aunt Emm, followed by one of Auntie Louie (which used up a great deal of the clay), and one of Mr. Hewitt.

The children chattered as they worked, and Miss Joyce walked around behind them, looking at what they were doing and making encouraging remarks. When she came to Charley, she stood silent for a moment behind her chair; then she said, with a kind of nervous bleat, "Oh, oh, they're *most* amusing! But they're not really anything to do with the story, are they?"

"Yes, they are," said Charley. "They're part of the five thousand."

Miss Joyce peered around at her uncertainly, almost as if she were afraid Charley might bite, and said with another little bleat, "Oh, oh! But you'll hardly be able to make all of them, will you?" She rested a finger in her cheek, thoughtfully. "I suppose you could make them in the front row, so to speak, and just sort of indicate the others behind them, couldn't you, with a larger lump?"

"On the contrary," said Charley. "These will be in the back row. There won't be any loaves or fishes left by the time it gets to them, and they'll starve to death."

Miss Joyce gave her one horrified glance and moved on, and Charley used up the rest of the clay to make a model of her, too. The girl she had met in the road sidled up to her and stood, gaping, as she was finishing it off.

"Hallo," said Charley, looking up.

"What's your name?" said the girl.

"Rowan. What's yours?"

"Marilyn." The girl scuffed her feet on the floor, then said, as if it were a set piece, "My mum, she say only tramps live under trees."

"Oh? What about gypsies, then?"

161

Marilyn shook her head. "My mum, she say gypsies live in trailers, round the scrap heaps. She say that were a lie what you said. No one don't live under trees. Only tramps."

"Nonsense," said Charley.

"Not without houses they don't."

"Well, I do."

"My mum, she say you don't."

"Well, I suppose I know where I live better than your mum," said Charley. "Anyway, I don't know your mum."

"No. And my mum don't know you. She say there ain't no such person."

"What, as me?" The girl nodded, solemn and owl-faced. Charley laughed bitterly. "Well, I don't have to ask your mum for permission to exist. Tell her I'll leave a plague of snails in her garden some night and get the birds to drop you-know-what on her washing; then she'll know whether I exist or not."

Marilyn looked half-scared. "Bor, and there was some on the piller slips last Monday! But then the birds does that quite often. That wasn't *you* made 'em do that."

"I'll tell them to drop more next time," said Charley confidently. "You'll see."

Miss Joyce clapped her hands for silence. Then she sat down at the piano and everyone stood up to sing. Charley, opening and shutting her mouth in time to the music, moved steadily backward toward the door as if she were playing Grandmother's Footsteps, and finally slipped outside. She had not known the words anyway, and there seemed nothing to stay for.

Outside, two women were waiting for their children. They stared after her as she went past, and she heard one of them say, "Well, she do look a proper scarecrow!"

"Right," said Charley to herself. "That proves what I always said. This dress is only fit for a scarecrow. Very well, Aunt Emm. You always said it was a nice dress. Now you can have it." And she marched off up the lane toward Mr. Bartlett's field.

19

Miss Joyce, the Vicar and the Scarecrow

When Miss Joyce followed the children out of the church hall a few minutes later, she looked around for some sign of the strange child. But she had gone. She talked to Marilyn Betts at the door for a moment or two, then shook her head and turned away toward the vicarage.

Mr. Bramwell, the vicar, was in the garden, examining his roses. He hurried to the gate.

"Well, did she turn up?"

Miss Joyce looked doubtful. "I think so—at least, I think she must have been the one you meant, but—"

"Legs covered in bruises, rather unkempt? But a bright, intelligent face? Lame, too. You couldn't possibly mistake her."

Miss Joyce looked startled. "Not lame, oh, no! This

one wasn't lame." Her usually good-natured face looked almost severe, Mr. Bramwell thought.

"Oh? What was she, then?"

"Well, perhaps a little—odd, simple, I don't really know. I asked Marilyn Betts afterwards and she had the same impression. Definitely."

"Oh? What did Marilyn Betts say?"

"She said she was nuts. Plain daft. The girl had told her she lived under a tree and had a hen house for a wardrobe."

Mr. Bramwell raised his eyebrows. "This sounds rather serious. A vagrant, perhaps? Did she give you that impression?"

Miss Joyce swallowed, then said rather harshly, "I think Marilyn was probably right. Anyway, she wasn't at all a desirable type. She struck me as being—well—vindictive."

"Ah." Mr. Bramwell fingered a rose, leaned forward to smell it, then turned to her again. "What was she wearing? A short skirt, very torn and dirty?"

"Good heavens, no! A long, green dress. Very long and very crumpled. And moldy shoes."

"What color hair?"

Miss Joyce made a gesture of impatience. "Really I hardly noticed. It was covered with a lot of weeds"— Mr. Bramwell's eyebrows went up again—"well, convolvulus—made into a sort of wreath. Really she looked quite extraordinary."

"Well, blow me down!" This time it was Miss Joyce's eyebrows which went up. "And she wasn't lame?"

"Definitely not."

"Nor scratched or bruised?"

"Not so far as I could see. I must say I didn't examine her too closely. I mean one hardly liked to stare, she looked so peculiar. And I had the other children to consider—"

He nodded. "Yes, yes, of course. It seems this must be another child. She didn't say I'd sent her?"

"No, and I must say I should have been surprised if you had. Now, if you'll forgive me, Mr. Bramwell, I ought to be getting along. I haven't cleared up in the hall yet—I knew you'd be wanting to hear as soon as possible—and Mother will be expecting me."

The vicar nodded again. "I'm sorry to have bothered you, Miss Joyce. My regards to your mother, and thank you for coming to tell me." He turned and went slowly into the house.

In the drawing room his wife was having tea with Miss Wetherall, the schoolmistress from Brinchester. Mr. Bramwell sat down, helped himself to a sandwich and waited for an opportunity to ask Miss Wetherall if she had met either of these two strange children.

Miss Wetherall had not. She looked interested and concerned. "A lame child, you say? And another who seems to be simple, and living rough on her own? How very strange! I can't say I've seen either of them." She paused, wrinkling her forehead. "I do remember, some days ago in Brinchester, coming across a child in a shop who appeared to be deaf. I noticed her because she was using signs only, pointing to what she wanted. I assumed she was deaf because clearly she couldn't speak, and it seemed such a pity her parents hadn't done something about it. They can do so much for deaf children these days, you know, teaching them to speak even when they have a total hearing loss. I may have told you about my friend Dorothy who works with—"

Mr. Bramwell interrupted. "Yes, I remember. Tell me, was this child very unkempt, scratched and bruised all down her legs? And very sunburnt?"

"Oh, no! Not at all."

"Not sunburnt? And you're sure not lame?"

"Oh, no. Certainly not lame, and not sunburnt either. Pale if anything. She looked like a town child to me."

Mr. Bramwell shook his head. "The one I'm interested in is quite distinctive. What concerns me about her is that I'm afraid she's being treated badly. All those bruises—and the fact that she won't tell me anything about herself and looks half-scared whenever I meet her. I realize now I was mistaken in not turning up this afternoon, but I thought, as she

167

seemed so unwilling to confide in me, Miss Joyce might have been able to get something out of her—who she was, where she lived, and so on."

"Oh, well, I expect we shall find out soon enough," said his wife, "though I must say, three strange children all turning up at once is a strange coincidence. But in a village this size none of them can remain unnoticed for long. Some more tea, Miss Wetherall? George, another sandwich?"

Mr. Bramwell took four without thinking. "I'll go and see Mrs. Denning tomorrow," he said thoughtfully. "She usually seems to know all that's going on."

Half an hour later, having cleaned up the paraphernalia of Sunday school and locked the church hall, Miss Joyce set off for home at Thornley. Pedaling past Mr. Bartlett's field on her bicycle, she was astonished to see the scarecrow leaning drunkenly sideways, with a bedraggled green dress hanging from its stick arms and a wreath of withered convolvulus pulled forward over its head.

Surely I've seen that before? she thought. *Can it be—Can it be—* She got off her bicycle, which was beginning to wobble, and moved nearer. Yes, there was no doubt of it—that dreadful child!—and how horribly she had stared at her while she was telling the story—it had been quite unnerving—It had been a trying afternoon, in any case—so hot—and now this. What did it mean? Could it be some sort of omen?

She had one of her nasty headaches coming on—she must hurry home. There was a threat of thunder in the air, and Mother would be waiting for tea. She remounted her bicycle and pedaling quickly but steering a little unsteadily, rode away. She never did feel quite herself when there was thunder about.

20

Someone to Talk to

Charley, too, had a headache. She had run all the way back from Mr. Bartlett's field in her under-clothes, and it had been fun—though she had thought she would die of heat and the excitement of not being caught before she got back. But now the excitement had worn off and she felt shivery and miserable. And lonely.

The day had gone all wrong. Her clergyman had never turned up although he had invited her. Miss Joyce had looked at her as though she were some strange kind of animal, probably dangerous. So had that silly girl. (Of course you had to play up to it when people looked at you like that.) And that silly girl's mum had said she didn't exist at all!

She longed for someone to talk to. The sun had

disappeared in a purplish haze, and it was very still in the copse. She wondered about the caravan, whether it was empty now. Perhaps the dog would be there alone.

She got up and tiptoed to the edge of the slope and looked down. All was quiet. Then she saw a stump of white tail and two small hind legs stretched out flat, below the projecting roof. They twitched slightly as flies worried them. It looked as if he were tied up and asleep. She waited for a while, then, as nothing stirred, slipped over the edge of the bank and let herself down gently on to the ground behind the caravan. She stood for a moment, not moving a muscle, her eyes fixed on the box of dog biscuits still standing on top of the meat safe, and hearing only the buzz of flies and mosquitoes. Then, very quietly, she crept round to the front.

The dog leaped up, his ears back, his eyes still glazed with sleep; then he recognized her and made small, subdued yelps of pleasure, whistling in his throat. She ran to him.

"Gosh, I'm pleased to see you! Are you pleased to see me?" She buried her face in his rough white coat and laughed softly in his ear while he twisted and turned, trying to lick her face.

There was a sudden sound of footsteps, and she shot around. A man with his face burned brown by the sun, and wearing an open-necked shirt and khaki shorts, had come up behind them. The dog leaped toward him joyfully, straining at the rope, and Charley scrambled to her feet.

"Hallo," he said. "Was it you who looked after my dog?"

She nodded, backing a few steps, surprised to see that he was not a boy after all, but a grown-up. "That was nice of you," he said. "I found your note. Did you think I'd abandoned him? As a matter of fact, someone else had."

"What, *left* him?"

He nodded. "I found him by the roadside about a week ago. Nobody knew him and nobody seemed to want him, so I brought him back here. It seemed a pity to leave him at the police station. I've had to be away in the daytime, working on a farm, but I've always got back in time for his supper and a walk." He seemed to be defending himself to Charley. "But I think he's enjoyed his holiday." He smiled. "Are you on holiday too? You look like it."

"Yes. Yes, I am."

"With your family?"

She shook her head. "I was sent to stay with my auntie—at least, she's not a proper aunt—" She watched as he knelt to untie the dog's rope. "Why did you tie him up?"

"In case he ran away," he said, fumbling with the knot. "Here—keep still, boy!"

"I ran away," Charley said, made suddenly reckless by the pleasure of talking to someone, "once," she added quickly.

"Did you?" He took her seriously, looking up at her while the dog jumped up and down impatiently, scrabbling and licking his chin. "Why did you do that?"

"Oh, I don't know—"

"And were you away a long time?"

Charley thought. "Nearly a week," she said.

He looked impressed. "What was it like?"

"Well, I've been—" She shook her head and started again. "I was scared quite a lot of the time. I wasn't very good at it. I don't think I made a proper job of it. It was a sort of cheat really—at least, it was in the beginning—" She stopped, afraid of saying too much.

He let the dog go free and stood up. "Did you have to do it?" he asked—sympathetically, as if running away were an unfortunate experience that might happen to anyone. She nodded. "Why?" Then, as she made no answer: "All right, we won't press that. Tell me where you go to school. Do you like it? What are you best at?"

Charley told him. He was the easiest person she had ever known to talk to, and before long she had told him all about school, and the others going to Spain, and Miss Watson's painting competition. Even—a little apologetically—about her prize.

173

"And are you using it?"

She nodded, her face lighting up. "Yes, here, I am. I couldn't at home."

He knew what she meant at once. "No, of course you couldn't. Not with everyone expecting you to produce a masterpiece! And it was after you won the prize that you ran away, was it?"

"Yes—well, after the end of term."

"And then you were sent away here?"

"Mmm."

He sat down on the step and stared thoughtfully at the ground in silence. Charley imagined he thought she had been sent away for a punishment, and was silent too, wondering how she could correct the impression.

"I'm running away, too," he said suddenly.

"You? You're not!"

"Yes, I am. I didn't know I was until just now. I told myself I was having a holiday, but now I know I'm really running away."

"What from?"

"Same as you."

"Same as me? Why, what—what was I running away from?" she asked, openmouthed.

He laughed. "Don't look as if you don't know! You told me yourself. All about Miss Whatsername and the painting—"

"But—"

"About how you knew she was expecting you to do something really good, and so you weren't going to try."

"I never said that!"

"You did, in so many words. You said you'd never be able to do it again."

"Well, I wouldn't.

"All right. Nobody's asking you to do it again. They're expecting you to do something different. And you're afraid you won't be able to, so you're running away. Aren't I right?"

Charley thought seriously. "In a way I think you might be. But that isn't what made me *actually* run away."

"What did?"

She shook her head. "It doesn't matter. I don't want to think about it. Go on about what you were saying. *Is* that running away? Not trying, I mean, in case you can't? Just forgetting about it?"

He nodded. "Probably."

"And is that what you're doing?"

"Yes, I'm afraid so."

"What ought you to be doing?"

"I ought to be at home, mugging up my work for next term. And when I think of next term, I'm so scared all I can do is run away and forget about it!"

Charley looked at him unbelievingly. "But you're not at *school?*"

"I am. Going to be. I'm going to my first teaching job."

"Golly!" This was a new idea, that even a teacher could be afraid of a new school, afraid of not living up to what was expected of him. She considered him seriously. "*You'll* be all right," she said.

"You don't think the kids will bully me?"

"No, I think they'll talk to you. I did. Though of course, I didn't know you were a teacher then."

"That restores my confidence," he said. "Talk to me some more. Tell me what you meant about not making a proper job of running away. Why was it a sort of cheat?"

Her face clouded over and she kicked at the sandy ground with her bare toe. "Well—I wasn't very far away from someone I knew, so it felt as if I belonged there."

"And where do you belong really?"

Charley opened her mouth, closed it, then found to her surprise that tears were welling up in her eyes. "I'm not sure," she mumbled.

"What do you mean, you're not sure?" His eyes widened suddenly. "I say! You're not still running away, are you? Are people looking for you?"

Charley recovered herself. "No," she said with absolute certainty. "No one's looking for me. I did think they might be, but now I know they're not. And they know I'm safe," she added. "I sent a postcard."

He looked unconvinced. "I'm not sure I like the sound of it," he said slowly. "I think I ought to do something about you, but I'm not sure what." He sounded worried.

Charley backed away a few steps. "It's all right. Really. Now."

"But where are you living? Who's looking after you?"

She moved back another step. "My auntie—"

"Does she live near?"

Charley nodded, then, without another word, turned and ran. She ran all the way around the outer edge of the copse, and it was not until a long while later that she dared creep back as far as the track in the bracken and through to her own camp. But he had not followed her.

She was annoyed with herself for having told him so much and letting him guess that she was still lost. She would have to keep out of his way now. But he was a nice man, she was sure, and it was comforting to know that he and the dog were there.

21

A Bottle of Milk

It was broad daylight when Charley awoke next morning. She had slept badly. Marilyn's face, leering at her and growing larger and larger, had recurred over and over again in her dreams, coming up close to hers and saying, "Tramps. Only tramps live under trees. Tramps. Tramps. *Tramps—*" until the word became sinister and terrifying and relentless, like tramping feet following after her and gaining on her, closer and closer, louder and louder. Each time the dream had become intolerable, she had awoken with a gasp and lain, trembling, while the tramping, grown distant and muffled, had gradually reduced itself to the throbbing inside her own head.

She lay low in her camp most of the morning and pottered about quietly, stowing her things away, then taking her suitcase a little farther up the slope and hiding it under a hawthorn bush. There was not much likelihood of the man finding her, but if he did it must not look as if she were doing more than just picnicking here in the daytime. But most likely he would have gone back to work anyway.

She risked going back to Holmdene once, to make sure Auntie Louie was still not there, half filled her bucket under the tap and came quickly away again. She could not have carried it full today. Her head ached and her face burned. Shudders ran up and down her spine, and she wondered whether she had what Aunt Emm called "a touch of the sun." The food bought in Frickham was finished. She was not hungry, but she had had no milk for days. Perhaps that was what she needed now. People always talked as if you would die if you didn't drink milk. She hoped they were wrong.

She counted the money in her purse and was shocked to find only four and tenpence left. How could that be? She thought she had been fairly careful in her planning. Then she remembered her rash spending in Frickham, after she had discovered no one was missing her at home. It had seemed unimportant then to be careful. If no one else cared, why should she? But she cared now. She would have to go easily with these last few shillings.

She set off for Brinchester, walking slowly. Thank

goodness there was no need to go as far as Frickham now she was not being searched for! She rested several times on the way and it was early afternoon by the time she arrived in the village. She went into the same small dairy as she had gone into on her first morning. How long ago that seemed! Someone was already at the counter, being served: a large woman with short-cut gray hair, wearing a gray linen dress. Her voice boomed through the little shop as she ordered butter and six eggs, and inquired after mister somebody's leg.

Charley waited in the background, dreading that she might be noticed and trying not to look at the luxuries she could no longer afford. Milk, and bread, and corned beef, she thought. *Not* ices, or fruit, or fizzy drinks. She took a bottle of milk from the crate by the door while waiting, and reached into her basket for her purse. It was not there. Nonsense, it must be! She felt again, not yet daring to look, but her hand came up against the wicker of the basket on all sides. In despair she looked, then went hot all over. The basket was empty. She had lost her purse. Now she had no money at all!

"Thank you, Miss Wetherall," the woman behind the counter was saying, "and will that be all?"

"Yes, thank you," said the large gray woman, picking up her things. "Isn't it incredibly hot! Quite overpowering. Good afternoon!"

Charley gave one terrified glance around, then, still clutching the bottle of milk, made a dash for the door. She heard a startled exclamation behind her and just had time to see the shopkeeper staring after

her, her eyes wide and outraged, and the large gray woman starting suddenly toward the door. Then she was outside in the street, running faster than she had ever run in her life before.

Her heart was thumping and her mouth dry with

181

fear as she pounded along. One or two people turned to stare curiously at her as she went thudding past them along the village street, but she never once glanced back. By now she felt sure she was being pursued by quite a large crowd.

Five hundred yards—and what seemed five hundred years—later, she swerved aside into a field of stubble and collapsed, panting, under the hedge. No footsteps sounded in the lane behind her. No sound of any kind disturbed the quiet afternoon other than a distant dog barking and her own rasping, gasping breath. She was safe. She had escaped. But she was a thief.

Now she could never go back to Brinchester. Everyone there would know. She might even be arrested—unless, of course, she could find her purse and go quickly back to pay for the bottle of milk. But that might be anywhere, probably in the fields she had cut across. She must get back to Market Barnham anyway. There, at any rate, no one would know. But what was she to eat? She had no money and nothing left but one small, hard lump of cheese. If only Ned had not gone away!

There had been a box of dog biscuits on the safe behind the caravan. Could one live on dog biscuits? She would not dare ask the man for anything. He was suspicious about her already, and if she asked for food, he would probably tell the police about her being lost. Then they would tell him she was wanted for stealing. She found she minded the idea of his knowing she was a thief even more than the idea of being hungry. If only there was someone else . . .

There was. She had forgotten the vicar. He had always looked kind. He had even seemed to want to get to know her—and she *had* been to his Sunday school. Perhaps, if she hung around near the vicarage, she might happen to meet him again. He might even ask her in to tea, to make up for not having been at Sunday school after he'd invited her.

She sprang up, recovered, though trembly about the knees, and hurried out into the lane and back toward Market Barnham. She would go around by way of the vicarage. No harm in being seen around there straightaway. She might have to pass the house several times before she was actually noticed. She picked some leaves and grasses to cover the bottle of milk in her basket, laid a few wild flowers on top to look more convincing, and hurried on. The sooner she left Brinchester well behind, the better.

As she turned into the road where the vicarage was, a car was just drawing up outside the gate. She hesitated on the corner, watching. Then, to her utter dismay, she saw the large woman in gray get out, lock the car door, and walk quickly up the path to the front door. Appalled, Charley turned and fled.

So the woman in gray had got there even before

she could! And she would be telling the vicar all about how Charley had stolen the milk. She must have driven here straight from the dairy—perhaps going to the police station first? Yes, there would have been time even for that.

So now, even here, Charley would be known as a thief! She would not dare go into another shop. Things were worse than she had imagined. She got back to her camp somehow, sank down, whimpering with exhaustion in the bracken, and opened the only thing she had brought back with her—the bottle of milk. The contents were solid and dark yellow and evil-smelling. The milk was not only sour, it had gone bad. It seemed like the last straw.

22

Truly Like Lizzie Scrotton

Gradually Charley pulled herself together. It was
no use crying over sour milk. She must eat, then she
would probably feel better. She unwrapped the remaining lump of cheese and nibbled it. She knew
now what the expression "hard cheese" really meant.
It was like trying to eat a fossil. But she washed it
down with water, and tried to think sensibly about
what she should do.

She must stay in the copse from now on, only
fetching her water very early in the mornings. She
would take some dog biscuits from behind the cara
van and eat those and there were still blackberries on
the hedges. Meanwhile, the man and his dog were
near at hand. She was not nearly so alone as she felt.
If only her eyes would focus properly (she kept

thinking she was seeing double) and her head would stop aching, things might not be so bad after all.

The cheese did make her feel better. She got up and picked and ate some blackberries, then decided she had better fetch the dog biscuits now, before the man came back from work. She would go the long way around instead of sliding over the bank; then, if he should happen to be there, he would not know where she had come from.

As soon as she came within sight of the caravan, she had a feeling that something was different. The dog was not outside, and she was disappointed, but something else was different as well. Then she realized what it was. The step was no longer in front of the door.

She drew nearer and saw that the curtains were pulled across, and the rope had gone from the hook inside the door. With a sinking feeling in the pit of her stomach she tiptoed around to the back. There was no sign of life. The meat safe, the box of dog biscuits, and the water cask had all disappeared.

She stood for a moment in the long grass, frowning and thinking; then she went around to the front again and tried the door. It was locked. She looked down and saw a round, light patch of yellowed grass at her feet, and wondered vaguely what had caused it. Then she remembered, it was where the dog's drinking bowl had stood.

So they had gone! The caravan was locked up, and clearly no one was coming back. She wondered why she had been upset about so small a thing as a bottle of sour milk. All the milk in Brinchester could not make up for the loneliness that descended on her now. There was a deathly stillness everywhere and the world seemed to have gone suddenly dark. The grass, the bushes, the trees were motionless, brooding, withdrawn into their own secret existence. She had thought herself part of them. Now she saw that they were nothing to do with her. They looked sinister and threatening. Adders would slip silently through the grass, poisonous fungi would sprout from the roots of the trees, and tramps might lie hidden under the bushes.

Slowly she went back into the copse. Now that she knew the caravan was deserted it felt different in here as well. The magic had gone. The quietness was menacing. And it was so dark! Why had she never realized it before? It was a hateful place. She must get out of it quickly.

She hurried to the place where she had hidden her things and plunged her hands into the bracken, feeling around for them, but they were not there. She felt panic rising inside her. She *must* find them. She scrabbled again, tearing her hands on a bramble, then, looking up, saw she was searching in the wrong place. She went on a little way, searched again, and pulled her basket and bundle of clothes out of the bracken. The suitcase, she remembered, was farther up, under the hawthorn bush.

How dark it had grown! She could hardly see at all now, and only found her case by feeling for it. There seemed no air left to breathe. It had been heavy and airless enough out in the open, but here it was stifling. Her head throbbed and felt as if it would burst. The bushes and undergrowth crowded in on her as she knelt in the bracken, fumbling at the locks of her case with trembling fingers. Twigs snapped suddenly and loudly, making her jump; then the silence fell deeper than before. She began to feel surrounded, suffocated, and frighteningly alone. Even the birds were silent.

Hurriedly she packed as much as she could in the case and stuffed the rest in the basket. Only one thing would not go in—it felt like her beret—and this she held tightly in her hand. As she got up to go, an enormous insect zoomed past her ear, hitting her hard on the cheek. It felt almost as big as a bird. She grabbed the suitcase in one hand, the basket in the other, and ran.

She was astonished when she came out into the open, to see what a change had come over the landscape. No wonder it had seemed so dark in the copse! The sun had gone. The sky was a lurid yellow color—almost brown—and over toward Thornley great black and purple clouds were banking up. Even as she looked, another mass of cloud began spreading over from the direction of Market Barnham, and she saw distant flashes of lightning.

Where was she to go? Nowhere was "home" now. The whole countryside looked dark and hostile. The thought flashed through her mind, *I'll phone home and tell Aunt Emm. She'll be furious, but at least she'll tell me what to do.* She tried to think where the nearest telephone box was, then realized she had no money. Anyway, it was too late. Aunt Emm would be in Southsea by now, Giles was away with the Barretts, and Mrs. Scrotton would be staying with her sister. Tears sprang to her eyes as she imagined the telephone bell ringing and ringing in the empty hall and no one answering.

She sat down weakly on her suitcase by the edge of the field and let the tears run. Now she was truly like Lizzie Scrotton.

She thought of the police station, that square redbrick house on the road to Frickham, but it was miles away. She would never get there tonight. She would go there first thing in the morning, though. She would confess, and tell them she was lost as well. Did children get sent to prison? She thought not, but they would have to do something with her. They couldn't turn her out to wander about the countryside, even if she was a thief. Perhaps, like Lizzie

Scrotton, she would be sent into a workhouse until Aunt Emm and Toby came home.

A low rumble of thunder made her leap to her feet, and lightning forked down in the distance. The panic rose again. "Help me!" she gasped out loud. And it was then that she remembered Mrs. Denning. She, at least, would be there. Ned had said she was a nice woman, "one of the old sort," whatever that meant. And she had a summerhouse in her garden.

She picked up the case and began running across the field. Now that she had thought of somewhere to go, she could not get there quickly enough. The sky was growing darker every minute and she realized with dismay that she was running straight into the storm—two storms, in fact, since the dark cloud that had started over Barnham was now meeting and merging with the purple blackness over Thornley.

Forked lightning pierced down repeatedly into the dark clump of trees behind Mrs. Denning's house. What if the house should be struck before she got there! It could not be helped. She had nowhere else to go. What if Mrs. Denning should see her and ask why she had come? To bring corncobs from Ned. But she had none. That had been days ago. Other vegetables, perhaps? You couldn't live only on corncobs. She could pretend she was bringing some other vegetables from Ned. But she had none. A message, then. Ned says he's sorry he's got no vegetables. They've got the blight . . .

Panting, she passed the haystack and the outhouses at the back of Bell Lane and turned into the cart track. The thunder boomed louder now and there was an uncanny yellow light over the fields. Her heart sank as she saw the deep purple blackness into which she was walking. Her head ached unbearably so that it was difficult to think sense. She wondered once or twice whether she could be dreaming; whether, if she lay down and closed her eyes, she wouldn't wake up later and find herself at home in bed. But she knew that would be dangerous, like falling asleep in snow.

She must think—think about anything. Mrs. Denning, then. I came to tell you Ned's sorry he hasn't any more corncobs. My dear child, how kind of you to come and tell me. Forgive my shutting the door, but it's thundering. I hope you won't get struck on the way back . . . No, that was wrong. Rub it out and start again. But I haven't got an eraser. Never mind, Charley, manage without one like the others do. Paint it out, then. Put a big black cloud in the picture. Oh, poor little dog! But it wasn't a dog. It was a fawn—her fawn, who had lived in the copse. But he didn't live there now. Tramps did. Why did she have to keep thinking about tramps? Think about Mrs. Denning . . .

She reached the gap in the hedge and went through into the field. A hot gust of wind blew up suddenly, filling her eyes with dust. She plunged

brownish-black, and greasy and torn. It can't be mine! she thought. It's an old tramp's cap! She dropped it in horror. But what did it matter now? She was a tramp herself, a thief, and a scarecrow. Anyway, it was useful. It would hold the turnip, which was thick with wet mud and too slippery to hold.

She was out of the field at last, and turning into the lane. A few more steps and she was at the gate. Then struggling up the drive. Now she was stumbling, slithering, across the lawn toward the summerhouse. Suppose it should be locked! But it was not. She leaned heavily against the door, which was stiff and creaked. It opened slowly, then swung wide with a rush, and exhausted and drenched, Charley fell sprawling on the floor.

23

A Stray Cat?

Mr. Bramwell got up and walked over to Mrs. Denning's window.

"It's looking extraordinarily dark outside," he said. "I think I'd better go before the storm breaks. It's been threatening for days. Once it starts, it'll probably go on all night."

Mrs. Denning nodded, collecting the teacups. "I'm glad you came," she said. "I'll certainly ask around about this child of yours. I'm surprised I haven't come across her already. You know, I'm sure I'm right about there being only one of them. The lameness might have been some temporary hurt, especially if she's been ill-treated, and the deafness may well have been not deafness at all, but dumbness, due to shyness—"

"She didn't strike me as being exactly shy," the vicar murmured.

"And Mildred Wetherall would naturally jump to the conclusion she was deaf," Mrs. Denning went on, "being so interested in the subject. Anyway, the second time she saw her—today—when she was actually taking the milk—well, the child would hardly be likely to say anything then, would she! What did Mildred say happened exactly?"

"She said she just took it and ran," said Mr. Bramwell. "And the pathetic thing was she'd taken it from a crate that was waiting to be collected, so it was probably sour! Mildred was quite worried about it. She'd hoped she might see her somewhere on the road, but when she didn't, she came straight over to tell me."

Mrs. Denning nodded briskly, at the same time filling a saucer with milk and crumbling a piece of bread into it. "As for Miss Joyce's account of her being peculiar—(No, my dear George, this isn't for you, it's for my stray cat. He usually turns up when the weather's bad)—well, we both know Miss Joyce is extremely conventional, and rather timid. And suppose the child *was* behaving in a peculiar way, surely that, too, could be put down to ill-treatment—" She broke off as lightning flashed across the sky. "Yes, go now. Or you'll be caught." She hurried him out into the hall, carrying the saucer with her.

A Stray Cat?

"You don't mind being left?" the vicar asked. "You're not nervous of storms?"

"Oh, no, I find them rather exciting! Anyway, there's John—I'm sorry he's in the bath. They keep extraordinary times, these young people."

"Of course, I forgot! Give him my regards and wish him luck. He'll be off soon, I suppose?"

"I suppose so," said Mrs. Denning. "*And* I shall miss him, but we won't go into that now—" She opened the front door, then jumped back in spite of herself as lightning forked down behind the trees, followed by a crack of thunder.

"You can see why I'm worried," said Mr. Bramwell, peering over her shoulder. "This girl—the one who came to Sunday school—according to Miss Joyce she told Marilyn Betts she lived under a tree. But where? And where on a night like this, for heaven's sake!"

He made a dash for his car, waved, and drove off. Lightning flashed across the fields, and as he turned into his own garage, the rain came thundering on the roof. It was not a fit night for a stray cat to be out, let alone a human being. He hoped, desperately, that the child had not been telling the truth.

Mrs. Denning stood by the door a moment, calling the cat, then put the saucer down by the step and went indoors. A little later, when the rain came, she went to the door again and looked out, but there was still no sign of it. She was worried—not only about the cat—cats could usually look after themselves—but about the strange child she had been hearing about. If it was true, it was terrible. Where was she now? Tomorrow she would start asking everyone, but it was hardly possible to do anything tonight, in weather like this. She went back into the sitting room and picked up her knitting, listening to the storm raging outside, and hearing from upstairs the comfortable, homelike sounds of splashing and singing as yet more hot water was run into the bath.

She sat up suddenly. Above the rushing sounds of rain and bath water she could have sworn she had heard another sound—a sort of soft, scrambling noise. The cat? She jumped up, ran to the door and peered out, but could see nothing through the screen of falling rain. The saucer of bread and milk appeared untouched though it was now flooded. She hesitated a moment, then shut the door again. Poor thing, perhaps it was hiding and would come back for it when she had gone. Meanwhile, she must get on. There was supper to prepare. The bath water was running away at last, and John was sure to be hungry again! She smiled to herself and hurried into the kitchen.

The storm lasted until the small hours. Once more that evening Mrs. Denning found time to glance out to see if there was any sign of the cat, but she waited only a moment—there was so much to talk to John about before he went away!—and she was convinced that the faint mewing she had thought she heard on first opening the door was only her imagination.

It was not until several hours later, when she awoke remembering she had not opened her window before getting into bed, that she heard distinct sounds of mewing—or was it whimpering?—and realized she had not imagined it. The storm had died away at last. She opened the window wide and leaned out. Faint sheet lightning still flickered in the distance, but there was no sound other than the dripping of the trees, and that strange other sound . . . She could hear it quite clearly now—a kind of mumbling whimpering going on and on, monotonously. *The summerhouse!* she thought. *It's in the summerhouse!* and snatched up her dressing gown.

Charley had no idea she had been talking and whimpering in her sleep. She had no idea of anything except that she was in a queer, muddled sort of dream, now running desperately through clogging mud, now lying in a dark hole on something so hard it made her bones ache. It was only when she heard a sudden startled exclamation almost in her ear, and looked up to see Mrs. Denning standing over her in a dressing gown, that she remembered vaguely where she was. Then she struggled to her feet.

"My dear child!" Mrs. Denning's voice was sharp

with anxiety. "Whatever are you doing here? I thought I heard something—"

Charley began to explain, talking quickly in a rambling, disjointed way. "They were after me—I had to—and it was thundering, and I thought I might be

struck dead—but I was hungry and I meant to pay for it, only I'd lost my purse, but there was only four and tenpence in it anyway—and it was sour after all. But I promised Ned I'd bring your vegetables—at least, he didn't ask me—" She tittered feebly. "But look," she staggered forward, holding out the cap, "here is your hat. I found it in the bracken. I'm sorry it got so wet but I expect it'll be all right. But you mustn't wear it tipped forward or you'll look like Aunt Emm and then people will laugh—"

She stopped, stared at the cap vacantly, then snatched it back. "Oh, no, I've made a mistake! This isn't your hat—I remember now it's a tramp's cap, it probably belonged to Lizzie Scrotton's father, only I don't think she had a father, so I don't know how that could have been . . . But this is what I was bringing you." She held out the turnip. "I'm sorry there's only one but you see Ned's away, so I had to steal that too, and—" Her voice faltered and her eyelids drooped. "And—and—" she swayed on her feet.

Mrs. Denning caught her, took her firmly in her arms, and staggered with her across the sodden, squelching lawn back into the house.

24

Mrs. Denning Takes Notes

The music was thin and sweet. It sounded like small footsteps running, then pausing, then running again. As Charley came up from the underworld of feverish terrors and nightmare, it reminded her of fine rain falling through leaves, or sunlight flickering on bracken fronds.

She stirred slightly, and found herself lying in such blissful comfort that she dared not open her eyes. It was a dream, of course—a heavenly beautiful dream. No wooden floor in a summerhouse—surely no bed, even?—could be as comfortable as what she was lying on now. And how else should there be music?

She lay, listening, her eyes still closed, and gradually the music grew clearer, taking shape; but this time it was not being played by a solitary wind instrument, but by a full orchestra. Behind her closed eyelids she felt herself growing more awake. Where could she be? What had happened? Ought she to be afraid?

"Anyway, it's the fawn's music," she murmured aloud.

"Yes."

She opened her eyes. Someone had said Yes, or was that a dream too? There was no one there. She heard a door close somewhere behind her, and saw in front of her a window surrounded by dark green leaves, and a sunset sky beyond. The pink glow of the sunset was reflected on the white wall beside her, and she saw that she was covered with a rose pink eiderdown. So it was a bed, after all! "Suffering codfish," she murmured, "some summerhouse," and fell promptly asleep.

When she awoke again, it was dark. Someone was sitting beside her, knitting under the light of a shaded lamp. It was Mrs. Denning. She leaned over Charley, saw that her eyes were open and said, "Good. That's better. Now I expect you're hungry." She stood up. "Bread and milk?" There was only the faintest question in her voice.

"Please," said Charley.

"Good," said Mrs. Denning again, and went out.

She was back in a surprisingly short time with a tray holding a bowl of steaming bread and milk, a spoon, and a large silver sugar castor. Beside the bowl lay a notebook with a small pencil attached. Charley set to work on the bread and milk, and Mrs. Denning sat watching her, with the notebook in her hand.

"Now," she said after a while, "let's hear all about it. First of all, who are you?"

Charley's mind flicked back over all the people she had been in the last seven days—Charley, whom Auntie Louie didn't want, a dumb girl, a princess, Lizzie Scrotton, a scarecrow in a green dress . . . She sighed and put down her spoon.

Mrs. Denning shook her head as if this would not do at all. "You'll have to tell me. I know you've run away, and for all I know you may have had very good reason, but it's gone quite far enough now. Someone must be getting pretty worried about you by this time."

"They're not," said Charley. "No one knows."

"Well, *I* know. And I think it only fair I should know who I'm entertaining. I'm Mrs. Denning, and I have a son called John. Now tell me your name?"

Charley thought again. "Rowan," she said slowly. (At least it was a pretty name. Ned had said so.)

Mrs. Denning appeared to agree. She smiled and wrote it down. "Rowan what?"

"Weston."

"Rowan Weston. You're sure?"

Charley nodded and Mrs. Denning smiled again. "Only you sounded a bit doubtful," she said. "And where do you live?"

Charley began to explain in stops and starts that she didn't live anywhere at present—at least, not until Auntie Louie came back. Or, if she didn't come back, then until Aunt Emm and Toby came back. Mrs. Denning put the notebook down on the tray and listened attentively.

"But where were you meant to be?" she asked at last.

"At Auntie Louie's," said Charley, leaning back on the pillow.

Mrs. Denning looked in the bowl, saw it was nearly empty, and said. "Enough?"

Charley nodded dreamily. "It was lovely."

"So you were meant to be at Auntie Louie's? And didn't you go?"

"Yes. Only by the time I got there she'd gone away," said Charley, her eyelids drooping. The bread and milk was making her drowsy.

Mrs. Denning looked at her hard for a moment, then said briskly, "Well, we won't go into all that tonight. I'll make you comfortable now and you can have another good sleep. We'll talk again in the morning."

Charley did not even remember being tucked up.

First thing in the morning Mrs. Denning came in

with a breakfast tray, and Charley's clothes hanging over her arm.

"All clean and dry," she said, "and after breakfast you can have a bath. Now, sit up and eat this. Start with the egg if you like. The cereal won't get cold."

Even having Mrs. Denning watch her while she ate could not quite spoil that breakfast for Charley. It tasted like the best meal she had ever eaten.

"You can get up afterwards," Mrs. Denning said. "Your temperature's gone down and the doctor says there's nothing much the matter with you, except some nasty bites and bruises, and probably a touch of the sun—nothing that a few days' rest and food won't put right, anyway. How are you feeling?"

This was a difficult question to answer. Charley thought, then said, "Surprised. I thought it was a dream at first."

Mrs. Denning laughed. "So did I when I found you in the summerhouse!"

"Has the doctor really been?"

"Yes, when you were flat out yesterday morning. And the police as well," Mrs. Denning added. Charley shot up in bed. "No, nothing to worry about, silly, but we had to let them know about you, naturally. We'd no idea who you were."

"Are they coming again?" Charley's voice was shaky.

"I shouldn't think so. Not if you tell me all I want

to know." She patted Charley's hand. "Are you still worrying about that bottle of milk? Because there's no need. It was waiting to be thrown away. I hope you didn't drink it!"

Charley sighed. All that was over now. Mrs. Denning picked up the notebook again. "Now, let's get to the bottom of all this. Auntie Louie lives—where?" Charley told her, adding that she was away. And where was Aunt Emm staying? Mrs. Denning asked. In Southsea, Charley told her. She couldn't remember the name of the guest house, but Aunt Emm's friend was Miss Cable. And Aunt Emm was Miss Raven. Her real name was Margaret, the Emm was for short, Charley explained. Mrs. Denning wrote it all down, and Charley's home address as well.

"Now," she said firmly, "tell me what happened when you got to Auntie Louie's."

"She wasn't there," said Charley. "She'd gone on holiday. There was a note left out for the milkman—" She paused, then added, "But I didn't go there straight away, so I suppose she thought I wasn't coming."

"How long was it before you went there?"

"About four days, I think."

"I see," said Mrs. Denning slowly, "I see . . ." She got up and walked over to the window and stood looking out on the lawn. She tapped the windowsill with her fingers, and then turned back to the bed.

"You know you've been a very naughty little girl, don't you?" she said.

"Yes, I suppose I have."

"And how long were you supposed to be staying with Auntie Louie?"

"Two weeks. Till Aunt Emm came back."

Mrs. Denning looked surprised, but all she said was, "Well, I can't go on scolding you forever. You *have* been very naughty, but I don't suppose it was all fun. Now what about this bath? I'll go and run it." She smiled at Charley and went out, calling to her a few minutes later that the bath was nearly ready and she had left a towel out.

Charley stepped out of bed with care, half expecting to feel thorns and prickles under her bare toes. Instead they sank into the soft pile of the carpet. She found she was wearing a long nightgown, much too large for her. She gathered it up over her arm, picked up her clean clothes, and tiptoed along to the bathroom. The luxury of quite ordinary things astonished her, the shining white tiles around the bath, the hot water gushing from the tap, and the large dry towel that Mrs. Denning had left out on a chair. She wondered how long it would take to get used to such things, and to the strange, enclosed, padded feeling of living in a house again.

She came out of the bathroom at last, pink all over, and feeling like someone quite different. Music was coming up from below—quick, joyful, lilting music. She stood for a moment, listening on the landing, then went quickly downstairs. The kitchen door was open, but Mrs. Denning was not there. The music was coming from another room, across the hall. The door was not quite shut. She pushed it a little and looked in.

A man was sitting in an easy chair turned toward the window. She could see only the top of his head, and his legs, and one hand raised, as if waiting for the final chords. As she hesitated in the doorway, wondering whether to go in, the music came to an end, and the man sprang up and went over to the record player.

"Oh!" said Charley.

He turned around in surprise, saw her and grinned. "Hallo," he said. "Come in. How did you like that? It was Haydn, in case you didn't know. You can't beat him for—" There was a sudden scrambling from under the sofa. "Hey Bogey! Gently old boy—" and a small white dog came bounding across the room and leaped up at Charley with yelps of delight.

25

Mother and Son

"You!" said Charley. "How—how did you know I was here?"

She patted the dog, who was still jumping up at her, and stared, amazed, at the man from the caravan. (Did Mrs. Denning know he was here? Was it really all right for him to be using the record player?) "Where's Mrs. Denning?" she asked in a low voice.

"Gone shopping," he said blandly. "She won't be long."

Charley shook her head confusedly. He did not seem nearly as surprised to see her as she was to see him. "How did you know I was here?" she repeated.

"I didn't. Not until my mother woke me up in the middle of the night saying look what I've found!"

"Your mother? Is Mrs. Denning your *mother?*"

He laughed at her astonishment. "She certainly is! And she asked me to keep an eye on you, and to give you some elevenses when you came down. What shall we have—coffee or chocolate?"

"Did you know it was me—when she found me in the summerhouse?" she asked, following him into the kitchen. "I don't remember any of it."

"Yes, of course. I recognized you at once. More easily than I can recognize you now." He grinned, looking down at her. "How was the bath?"

"Super. It felt awfully queer. Everything feels queer. Sort of soft—and muffled—and shut in."

He nodded, reaching for the saucepan. "Upholstered. I know. It always feels like that to me when I've been camping. It must feel even queerer to you, judging by the state you were in when you arrived. Where on earth have you been living, you silly little chump? You had me worried, you know." He poured milk into the saucepan. "Say which, coffee or chocolate?"

"Chocolate."

"Good. Same for me too, then. It's easier." He took down two mugs and fetched the tin from the larder. Charley watched as he put sugar into the bottom of the mugs.

"Why did you go away?" she asked.

He turned to look at her. "Did you go back to the

caravan, then? After I'd gone?" She nodded. "And found it locked up? What then?"

"It was terrible—" She shuddered, remembering the horror of it. "And I was lonely," she added.

"Oh, shame. I thought I'd frightened you clean away. I thought you'd probably gone back to Auntie. I searched ages for you; then I thought I'd better come home myself. It was high time I did. I was having a sort of last quiet fling on my own, until you reminded me I was running away! Old Bartlett had lent me the caravan and I was rather enjoying the work on the farm but—well, really I should have come back before. Anyway, I packed up that same night, went to the farm next morning, then collected my traps, *plus* Bogey, and got back here about tea-time—lucky, as it turned out, with that storm brewing up—and Lord, what a welcome we got!" He laughed. "My mother took one look at me and bundled me straight upstairs into the bath. She'd got the vicar coming to tea. Funny thing was, I discovered later he'd come specially to tell Mum about you. Seemed to think there were three of you or something. He'd got you properly on his mind."

He fetched a tin of biscuits from the cupboard and they sat at the kitchen table, drinking chocolate and munching, while the dog waited hopefully, staring at the biscuit tin.

"Why did you call him Bogey?" Charley asked.

"Because of the way my mother looked at him when she first saw him," he said, laughing. "She's got some stray cat she's been feeding, and seemed to think he would eat it." But Bogey was the gentlest chap, he told her—wouldn't even chase a rabbit. They'd taken him out shooting on the marsh one night—he and young Bartlett—and he'd enjoyed the run but hadn't got a clue about retrieving. "I'm hoping my mother will keep him," he said. "He'd be good company for her when she's alone again. I should have come home before, of course, it's hard on the old lady—she's the best mother in the world, but . . ."

"But what?"

He smiled. "I never can make her understand I'm not a little boy anymore. She's still got the idea I need feeding up, and when I'm away, she worries about me. She loves me too much," he said, with a rueful shake of the head. It seemed a strange thing to be regretful about, Charley thought.

Mrs. Denning came back with the shopping and immediately there was a bustle. The table was cleared, the shopping unpacked, John was set to wash up the mugs and peel potatoes, and Charley helped to cut the runner beans.

There was a lot to be done after lunch, Mrs. Den-

213

ning said. Aunt Emm must be got in touch with—it shouldn't be too difficult to discover which guest house was being run by a Miss Cable. The police were always very cooperative. Rowan's things must be unpacked and gone through properly (perhaps she would like to help with the washing?), and John must get down to work straight away. Did Rowan know he'd been on holiday in Devon, camping?

John looked a little shamefaced at this and said, "Yes, and I had a good time. Actually, I had a short spell in old Bartlett's caravan as well, on the way back. It seemed a pity to waste the good weather."

His mother gave him a quick, surprised glance, then bustled about, fetching saucepans from the rack and filling them at the sink. One fell with a clatter to the floor. She picked it up quickly, held it under the running tap, then clapped it down on the draining board.

"And when will you be leaving?" she said, apparently casually, with her back still turned.

"Thursday or Friday, next week."

"So you'll only be here about ten days?"

"Afraid so, Mum. But I'll be back at half term."

Charley slipped out of the kitchen. She had an uncomfortable feeling that she ought not to be there. Mrs. Denning had looked put out, though her voice had sounded calm enough. Anyway, there was something she wanted to do before her washing was gone through. She ran upstairs, took the strip from Auntie Louie's letter out of her suitcase, and put it in her pocket. It was not for other people to read.

When she came down again, Mrs. Denning and John were talking quietly together in the kitchen.

"I feel like writing a stiff letter to this Auntie Louie person," Mrs. Denning was saying. Charley stepped back quickly from the open door. "I can't think what she was playing at, going off on holiday like that when she was expecting the child to turn up."

"But you forget Rowan didn't turn up," said John.

"I don't forget at all," said his mother sharply. "But does it make sense, to go off without doing anything about it, when a child of that age hasn't turned up? She ought to be ashamed of herself."

"But it wasn't her fault!" said Charley, suddenly bursting into the room. "She isn't usually like that at all. She was busy—she told Aunt Emm she was. You can't blame her!"

Mrs. Denning pursed up her lips and said nothing. She had not meant Charley to overhear. But John was interested. "Who do you think was to blame, then?" he asked.

"Aunt Emm, of course."

"But she couldn't have meant to send you away to fend for yourself," said Mrs. Denning reasonably.

"She sent me to Auntie Louie's when she knew she was busy and couldn't really do with me. You don't know Aunt Emm. She's a—hateful old trout."

"You shouldn't talk about her like that, whatever you may think she's done," said Mrs. Denning. "She's a relation, after all."

"She's Dad's relation as well," said Charley defiantly, "and he called her that. He told Mother the old trout meant well even if she wasn't everyone's cup of tea."

Mrs. Denning looked quickly at her son, as if daring him to laugh, but John's face was hidden behind the newspaper. "I think it's time we had lunch," she said firmly.

"But she *doesn't* mean well," said Charley, determined to have the last word where Aunt Emm was concerned.

26

Auntie Louie's Letter

Aunt Emm came.

The following afternoon Charley heard her voice in the hall. Mrs. Denning opened the door, saying, "Ah, Miss Raven! Come in," and led her through to the sitting room.

"I came as soon as I could—it's *most* unfortunate—I had to leave the little boy with my friend in Southsea. The police said—" The sitting-room door closed behind them.

Once more Charley found herself wondering what was being said about her behind a closed door, but this time she was more interested in what Aunt Emm might be saying, rather than what she might be hearing. She looked at herself in the bathroom mirror, put out her tongue at herself to show she didn't care what was being said, and went downstairs.

Aunt Emm sprang to her feet as soon as Charley came in. "Oh, Charley, you naughty, naughty girl!

How *could* you do such a thing?" She looked quite different. Her face was grayish and had gone into hard little creases. Charley was shocked at the change in her.

"But what—" she began.

Aunt Emm shook her by the arm impatiently. "We never even guessed anything was wrong until Giles got that extraordinary postcard from you. He sent it on to me because he didn't know what to make of it—it came just before the police came—he said he thought you must be dotty"— old, familiar words, sounding strangely in this new place! "—and you didn't send *that* until you'd been away three days. Three whole days!"

"Four," Charley corrected. "But I *did* send it. And I said I was quite all right."

"Yes, but you should never have been there at all! You should have come home at once, as soon as you found Auntie Louie wasn't there. At least you should have phoned home, or gone next door or something—"

"I couldn't have. It was the middle of the night."

"What are you talking about, you silly child? The coach got to Market Barnham at twelve thirty. You'd have got to the Hewitts' at one, at the latest, even if you'd dawdled."

"Do you mean"— Charley was staring at her with hatred and amazement in her eyes—"do you mean she wasn't *ever there*? And *yet* you sent me?"

Aunt Emm looked exasperated. "Don't be so silly, Charley! You know very well we didn't know that at the time, or of course you'd never have been sent."

"You knew she didn't want me," said Charley, in a low, accusing voice.

"Nonsense. I didn't know anything of the sort."

"You're a liar," said Charley, loudly and clearly.

Aunt Emm's mouth hardened and she turned to Mrs. Denning. "You see what I mean?" she said, flinging out her hands.

Mrs. Denning said, "Come here, Rowan." Charley hesitated, then went and stood beside her chair. "Why did you say that?" asked Mrs. Denning, looking up at her. "It was extremely rude."

Charley gave one furious little gasp and looked as if she were about to fly at Aunt Emm, but Mrs. Denning seized her by the hand and held it firmly. "Why did you say that?" she repeated. "There must be some reason. What made you think the Hewitts didn't want you?"

Charley, with her mouth firmly shut, reached in her pocket and brought out the strip off Auntie Louie's letter, so worn and limp now that it was almost in pieces.

Mrs. Denning read it without a word, then handed it over to Aunt Emm, still holding Charley firmly with the other hand.

Aunt Emm read it with a puzzled face, then turned it over. "Why, it's the address! I gave you that in the coach. It came off her letter." She frowned and read it again. "But—wait a minute, I may have got the rest of it here still." She fumbled in her bag and produced the rest of the letter, read quickly down the page, then handed it, and the torn strip, over to Mrs. Denning, with a look that was almost malicious in its triumph.

Mrs. Denning read aloud:

Dear Miss Raven,

Ever so sorry to hear about young Toby and would have liked to help if I could. It's a bit difficult though about having Charley as I'm working full time now and she'd be on her own more than I'd like. It's not that—

Mrs. Denning had reached the bottom of the page and turned to read from the torn strip:

I don't want Charley. You know that. It's the work. Really I've got my hands full already. If it could be arranged though that I could go part time that would suit fine. I liked having her here before and know she's easy enough. I'll ask at the works and sure they'll oblige. We're going to Hunstanton early October so it'd fit nicely but I'd be obliged if you could confirm when settled as Reg's sister is due to go into hospital soon with her leg and they never say when, do they.

Yours truly,
Louise Hewitt

"There!" said Aunt Emm with a triumphant smile.

Mrs. Denning did not smile back. "And you did 'confirm when settled,' I suppose?"

"Of course I did! Let me see, now, what did I say?" Aunt Emm frowned into her lap, thinking. "I said I was *most* grateful for her suggestion of working part time, as it was a problem knowing what to do with Charley. That I knew she was very busy, and as time was getting short, I would take it as settled the child was to come unless she telephoned (reversing the charge, of course. I remember I definitely said that), or sent a telegram. I told her Charley would take the coach arriving at Market Barnham at twelve thirty on the Tuesday—that I myself would see her off—and there was no need for her to be met as she knew the way there, and knew where the key was kept if they were out—I'd already made sure of that, of course. I even mentioned that Charley would be bringing a packed lunch with her, so wouldn't need anything further until teatime, or whatever they call their evening meal—" It sounded almost as if Aunt Emm was boasting about all the things she had done. Charley felt embarrassed for her.

"And I ended up by thanking her most civilly for all the trouble she was taking," said Aunt Emm, and sat back with hands folded in her lap, almost as if waiting for applause.

"Everything, in fact, arranged for Rowan's—Charley's comfort," said Mrs. Denning, looking her straight in the eyes.

"Well, of course! I do the best I can," said Aunt Emm, looking startled.

"And Mrs. Hewitt didn't answer that letter?"

"No, but I told you, she was very busy."

"I see," said Mrs. Denning. She turned to Charley. "You see, Rowan? It wasn't that she didn't want you. You were too ready to jump to conclusions, weren't you? It's a silly thing to do sometimes."

"I suppose so," Charley mumbled, trying not to show her tremendous relief at knowing Auntie Louie *had* wanted her. "But she might not have."

Aunt Emm jumped up. The next thing to be done, without doubt, was to find out what on earth Mrs. Hewitt was thinking of. It was disgraceful that she should have let everyone down like this. Aunt Emm would go around there at once—Charley had better come with her; it was not fair that Mrs. Denning's kindness should be taken advantage of—Mrs. Denning said no, Charley should stay and have her rest, the doctor had ordered it. It was a nice day, so she could have it in the garden. In any case, she asked, was it really worth Miss Raven's while, as the Hewitts were away? Yes, it was, said Aunt Emm. There must be *some* way of finding out—perhaps the post office . . . She collected her things together, and, refusing Mrs. Denning's offer of a lift, set off straightaway to walk to Holmdene.

Mrs. Denning became busy immediately. She must

make scones for tea. She would take John some coffee up in his room. He was working, she was glad to say. As for Charley, it was time for her rest. She would find a rug and cushions in the cupboard under the stairs. Charley could tell by her manner that she was feeling kindly toward her, but did not want to discuss Aunt Emm with her just now.

the trees that had been like silent enemies, the threat of tramps, and adders, and was lying once more under her rowan tree, hearing the thin whispering of the leaves overhead, and watching her fawn as it stepped delicately through the bracken, lightly lifting its head to sniff the air, then danced across the sunlit clearing, away into the trees. She shivered with pleasure as it all came back. It had been magical—the music as well—and it belonged to her alone.

The record came to an end. She heard footsteps behind her, and opened her eyes. John stood there, smiling.

"The fawn's music," he said.

She sat up suddenly, staring at him.

"What's up?" he said, surprised. "I thought you liked it."

"How did you know?" she whispered.

"Know what, that you liked it? It was the first thing you said, when you woke up, don't you remember? You said, anyway it's the fawn's music, so naturally I supposed you liked it."

"Where did it come from?" she asked uncertainly. "Was it you with the record player, that time when I woke up?"

"Yes, of course."

"But why did you say it was a fawn's music?" she asked, trying now to sound casual.

"Well, it is. You recognized it yourself—*L'Après-*

Midi d'un Faune, by Debussy. I thought he might be your special for the moment. I thought perhaps music was your line."

She looked blank, shaking her head. "What does it mean? I'm not very good at French. Afternoon something?"

"Yes, 'Afternoon of a Faun'—I suppose that's what you might call a literal translation. Why so surprised?"

"I—I used to hear it in the copse," Charley mumbled cautiously. She had an uncomfortable feeling that something precious was about to be destroyed, but did not know how to prevent it.

It was. John's sudden laugh was enough to do that. "Good lord, did you hear it there, too? That was me trying to play it on my flute. It seemed such a wonderful chance to play it over and over again without driving everyone round the bend! I never imagined I'd be overheard!" He laughed again, a little self-consciously. But Charley could not smile.

"I think I am hungry after all," she said.

"Right, I'll go and see what's in the cupboard." And he went back into the house, as she had hoped he would.

She sat hugging her knees, humped and heavy with disillusionment. So that was all it had been! John in the caravan, learning to play a piece on the flute, whereas she had imagined—what had she imag-

227

ined? It did not matter now. A secret, golden world had fallen to pieces. It was as though a picture had fallen from the wall and smashed to smithereens, and the world of the picture had turned out to be nothing but an old piece of paper with paint marks on it, and a cardboard backing. It's no use now, Aunt Emm would have said. The glass is broken. And John Denning, of all people, had broken the glass. *He's no better than Aunt Emm*, she thought bitterly.

But she tried to look as if nothing had happened when he came back with a packet of biscuits and two glasses of orange squash. Nothing *had* happened really. He had done no more than anyone else did when they spoiled something for you without knowing. And he was kind.

He said, sitting down beside her, "That copse was a pretty good place, wasn't it? I used to think there was something almost magical about it, sitting out there in the evenings just before it got dark. I"— he glanced at her—"I'm sorry if I spoiled it for you."

"You didn't," she said quickly. "It was a horrible place anyway."

"Oh, come—"

"In the end, it was." She took a biscuit and nibbled it, but shook her head when he offered her the orange squash. "I had too much. I drank it all that week."

"What was it like, that week?" he asked.

She told him. About hen house corner, and Ned, and going into Frickham, and her fright about the burning stubble and the men with the gun! Then about running to Holmdene in the middle of the night and finding no one there.

He listened seriously. "And you were pretty scared?"

She nodded. "Terrified. You see, before, the police had been looking for me (at least, I thought they were), and that was awful—like being hunted. But afterwards, when I found they weren't, it was worse. I didn't belong anywhere then."

"You're a lot braver than I am," he said. She looked at him in surprise. "Yes, you are. You were frightened of running away and yet you tried to. You did, in fact—though, mind you, it's not a good thing to do—but to me, it was the easiest thing in the world. I didn't have to be brave to do it." He got up. "How are you getting on with my mother?"

"I like her," said Charley.

"So do I." He smiled. "I'd better get back to work now, before your aunt comes back. The old lady wants me out of the way in case I say too much!"

She heard him shut the door of his room, and then she, too, went into the house, trailing her rug.

Aunt Emm came back, hot, dusty, and full of complaints about the unmade-up roads, but satisfied with what she had discovered. As she had suspected,

the Hewitts had gone off at a moment's notice
—*without* telephoning, of course—the day before
Charley was due to arrive. Aunt Emm had gone
around the back of the house (where, incidentally,
she had seen something *suspiciously* like the remains
of the fruitcake she had sent lying by the scullery
window—the wastefulness!) and had managed at last
to attract the attention of their next-door neighbor—a
most disagreeable old woman. She had gathered
from her that some relative had gone into hospital,
and the Hewitts were going to look after her place
while she was away. Mrs. Hewitt had not—according
to Mrs. Wilks—said anything about expecting a child
to stay, which only went to show . . .

"To show what?" Mrs. Denning murmured, but
Aunt Emm merely stared at her and went on with
her story. She had managed, after a great deal of
trouble, to persuade Mrs. Wilks to let her have the
key of Holmdene, though Mrs. Wilks had insisted on
going with her (as if she would want to steal anything from that house!) and it had taken an uncon-
scionable time because Mrs. Wilks was not only deaf,
but lame and grossly overweight as well, and had
grumbled all the way. However—they had, at last,
succeeded in opening the door, and there—*just* as one
might have expected—was Aunt Emm's letter lying
on the mat. Unopened!

"But they couldn't open it if they weren't there," Charley interrupted.

"*Unopened*," Aunt Emm repeated, "and here it is!" She took it out of her bag and waved it in front of Mrs. Denning as if its actual existence were proof of her own blamelessness.

"But I never doubted you had written it!" said Mrs. Denning in surprise. "I'm sorry if I gave that impression. Did you notice the postmark, by the way? Is it readable?"

Aunt Emm peered at it, looked confused, then peered again. Mrs. Denning looked. Neither of them said anything.

"What does it say?" asked Charley.

Mrs. Denning moved away to look out of the window, and Aunt Emm turned on Charley, suddenly furious. "Did I give it to *you* to post? I did, didn't I? I must have."

"No, you didn't," said Charley.

"Are you sure? It must have been Mrs. Scrotton, then."

"I didn't think you ever gave Mrs. Scrotton letters to post," said Charley.

Mrs. Denning came back. "It doesn't matter now," she said quickly. "Mistakes do happen sometimes. I suggest we forget about it and have tea. You must be ready for it after your long walk, Miss Raven."

But Aunt Emm was not to be put off. "I don't think a thing like this should be dropped," she said. "*Someone* must be to blame."

There was a second's silence; then Mrs. Denning said, "Very well, if you insist on someone being to blame, we'd better go into it thoroughly. This letter, apparently, was posted on the Saturday, three days before Rowan was due to arrive. That means either that someone forgot to post it, or that it wasn't written until then—possibly the evening before and posted next day. If it was as late as that, it's obvious it didn't leave enough time to make sure of its arrival. Mrs. Hewitt's letter asking you to confirm the arrangement, was written—as far as I remember—at least a week before that. When she didn't hear from you, she clearly thought you'd make other arrangements for Rowan, and when the call came from Hunstanton—on the Monday, wasn't it?—she naturally went straightaway. Probably just before this letter arrived. Now, only you, Miss Raven, know when you wrote it. Can you remember?"

Aunt Emm frowned, trying to think back.

"There's one way to find out," said Mrs. Denning, "and that is to open it and see. I imagine you'll have dated it. But, as I said, I think we'd better have tea now. It is ready." And she made for the door.

A flicker of doubt crossed Aunt Emm's face for an instant. She stood uncertainly, fingering the letter, then put it back in her handbag and closed it with a snap.

"Yes, perhaps you're right, Mrs. Denning. I could certainly do with some tea now. It was farther than I'd thought, you know, and I hadn't realized so many of these country roads were *still* not properly . . ."

They went in to tea.

28

Aunt Emm

Aunt Emm was looking tired, ill, and dispirited. She talked a great deal over tea about how much there had been to do, how difficult it was, running someone else's household, and how—no matter how carefully you made arrangements—someone, or something, was bound to upset them.

To Charley's surprise, Mrs. Denning agreed. It was a shame, she said, that Aunt Emm's holiday should have been spoiled. She was sure she needed one more than ever now after all the worry, and if she would consider going back to Southsea for the remaining week, Mrs. Denning would be only too happy to have Charley stay on with her.

Charley held her breath while Aunt Emm protested that it was out of the question. But Mrs.

Denning insisted, and finally it was arranged that Aunt Emm should stay the night and leave early the next day. John would drive her to the station at King's Lynn to see her off. Charley was delighted.

Aunt Emm came in to see her when she was in bed that evening. "Well, Charley, I'll be off in the morning, so I'll say good-bye now."

"Yes," said Charley. "Good-bye."

"It's all been very unfortunate," said Aunt Emm, looking vaguely around the room, "but Mrs. Denning has been very kind. I haven't had time to go through your clothes very thoroughly, but it looks as though you need some new pajamas. And I can't see your best dress anywhere—it's most extraordinary. Your vest needs a mend, too, I see." She picked it up and examined it while Charley sat up in bed, wishing she would go.

"However, we'll have to leave all that till you get back," said Aunt Emm, putting the vest down again. "I'm making arrangements to come and fetch you myself when we get back from Southsea, so you won't need any money for your fare."

She looked as uneasy as Charley felt, and seemed to be talking so as to avoid having to say anything. When at last, after a hasty peck on the cheek, she went out, closing the door behind her, Charley lay down with a sigh of relief.

How awful to be Aunt Emm, she thought. Aunt

Emm, with her ladies' hats and her near mustache, always shopping, or mending underclothes, or making arrangements. No fawn, no magic, no secret world of her own . . . But what about Charley's secret world? Had John really destroyed it? She hummed the familiar phrase of the fawn's music over quietly to herself, and realized that nothing was changed. It didn't matter if it had only been John playing the flute. Perhaps she *had* thought that was real magic, but it still reminded her of the copse, the way it had always been until that last day, and she knew that nothing had been destroyed. The music had only made it better. And the dark side of that secret world—the snakes slithering through the grass, the tramps lurking in the undergrowth, the suffocating feeling of the bushes crowding in on her—that, too, had probably been mostly her own imagination. But that had not made it seem any less terrible. It seemed as if so much, both beautiful and terrible, was really inside herself . . . *But I'd rather risk being scared to death*, she thought, *than have to live like Aunt Emm with nothing but things and things and things* . . .

She was just dozing off when she heard voices under the window. She opened her eyes. Mrs. Denning and Aunt Emm were walking in the garden. Broken snatches of their conversation drifted up to her. Aunt Emm's voice—"always so difficult . . . other people's children . . ." and Mrs. Denning's in reply, "I understand you were a matron in a prep school for some years?" The voices receded and became a murmur. Charley closed her eyes again. Aunt Emm would be telling Mrs. Denning all about how wonderful the boys were, and how wonderfully she had managed them, and what a wonderful school it had been. She had heard it all before.

The voices grew louder again as they came back toward the house. There was a scraping of wood on stone as they settled down in deck chairs on the veranda. "I never could do with girls"—it was Aunt Emm again—"I never did understand them." Charley raised herself on one elbow to listen. "I only had brothers, you see, four of them. I got on very well with them—I had to, I suppose—but somehow we never seemed to come across girls. I'm afraid we rather scorned them." (An inaudible murmur from Mrs. Denning.) "But it's all so different nowadays. They're treated the same as their brothers, they have the same opportunities, the same education, even the same clothes. My nephew's always been so particular about that—that she should have just the same as the others—jeans, parkas, things like that. No difference made at all. She doesn't realize how lucky she is. I always had to go around in skirts—except when we were at the seaside, of course, when I was allowed to wear shorts—"

The idea of Aunt Emm wearing shorts was so

astonishing that Charley had to bury her head in the pillow for a moment. (It might not have been so funny if she had not automatically imagined Aunt Emm as wearing her hat as well.)

"Nor any question of being expected to help with the baking or the ironing, the way I had to," Aunt Emm was saying, when she lifted her head again. "I assure you she's never been treated in any way differently from the boys. Really, she's been quite spoiled, I think."

There was silence for a moment; then Mrs. Denning said, "What about other clothes—party dresses, for instance—she's had those?"

"Well, there you are! She had a best dress—which seems now to have quite disappeared—but she always made the most awful fuss about wearing it. It was a very nice dress, not exactly a *party* dress—but I can't imagine her consenting to wear anything like that even if it was bought for her—but it was tasteful and sensible, in a nice shade of green ["It wasn't," Charley murmured, "it was sick green"], perfectly adequate for any special occasion. I can't think what's happened to it . . ."

"It must have been difficult for you," Mrs. Denning said thoughtfully, "being the only girl amongst so many boys."

"Oh, I don't know—"

"Did you never miss the sort of things girls like? Pretty things?"

Aunt Emm gave her own particular laugh, which was short, sharp, and explosive—more like a bark which had escaped by accident. "Oh dear, no, I soon had that knocked out of me! I suppose there was a time when I would have liked frills and fancy things, when I was much younger"—she barked again—"I remember once hankering after a mauve satin handkerchief sachet, of all things. One of my cousins had been given one. But I was soon laughed out of that! In any case, there wasn't much money to waste on such things, what with the boys' education, and so on ..." their voices drifted away.

How strange, thought Charley, nearly asleep, Aunt Emm never could do with girls ... "I'm afraid we rather scorned them" ... but hadn't Aunt Emm been a girl herself? ... Or was that why she so nearly had a mustache. ...

29

The Holiday Task

Aunt Emm had gone by the time Charley came down next morning. Mrs. Denning said John had overslept, but they had just made it, and she had caught the train with two minutes to spare. Charley said, "Good," then happily forgot all about her. There was so much else to think about.

Several pleasant things happened during the next few days. One was a letter from Auntie Louie, which was better than anything Charley could have hoped for, beginning *"My poor lamb, what a dreadful thing to have happened, I cried like a baby when I heard,"* and ending with *"Mr. Hewitt says he never would have wished such a thing on any child and it's really boys he isn't so keen on, so if I play my cards right I expect you'll get a proper invitation next time, who knows?"*

Another thing was a card from Giles, saying, "I

never thought you'd really do it. It was dotty. But Peter B. says you must have got some guts. What was it like?" Charley treasured this. To have Giles interested in her!

Mrs. Denning, looking for the green dress that Aunt Emm had been so concerned about, and learning at last what had happened to it, decided the best thing to do would be to buy a new one. She and Charley went into Welston and spent a tiring but satisfactory afternoon, looking at dresses, and finally choosing the sort of dress which Aunt Emm would never have chosen, but which Charley, secretly, rather admired herself in. It was not green. It was not any one color more than another, but there were flashes of reddish orange in it, the color of rowan berries. When Charley came back wearing it, John agreed with his mother that it suited her so well it must certainly be a present from both of them. "If Miss Raven allows," Mrs. Denning said. Altogether it was a happy week.

The day before John was leaving for his new job, he and Charley were on the veranda, watching Bogey as he tore up and down after the ball John was throwing for him. Every now and then, Bogey stopped and began digging holes in the lawn with ferocious energy, throwing out the earth behind him with his back paws, and each time, John got up, fetched the ball, and threw it again.

"Not that it really matters," he said, "now Mum's decided to keep him. I think he'll get away with more than either of us could, in the end." He sank down in a deck chair and stretched out his legs. "What luxury! And to think that tomorrow I'll be a schoolmaster, learning all the kids' names, and nagging them for their prep. By the way, what about yours?"

"My what?"

"Your holiday task for Miss Whatsername?"

She shook her head. "I'm not doing it. I didn't have to."

"Fair enough," he said. He sat up suddenly. "I say, what about the paintings you were doing in the copse—you didn't leave them there, did you, in all that rain?"

"No, they're upstairs. But they're not really paintings. It's just things I did in a book, as I went along."

"Could you bear to show me?"

"Not really."

"Fair enough," he said again.

But a little later, she brought down the paint box to show him—"It's a bit of a mess now," she said, "but you can see it's a good one"—and because he didn't ask again, she suddenly changed her mind and produced the sketchbook as well. "You can look if you like," she said casually, putting it down beside him.

"Thanks," he said, equally casually, still admiring the paint box. "I say, it is a good one! You've got rose madder, and viridian, and aureolin, all sorts of swish colors I never had in mine."

"I know. They're real artist's colors. The only other thing I ever had like it was a bottle of Indian ink Dad gave me, but I upset it in bed, so I never got another." She laughed and ran off down the garden with Bogey. She could not have borne to be there while he looked at the book.

But a few minutes later he shouted to her. "Rowan, come here!" She went back. "You are a chump! This *is* your holiday task. Whatever else? I think it's splendid. All about a girl and a fawn—it *is* a fawn, isn't it?" She nodded. "I like this one of him going up the long, empty road—it's the cart track, isn't it? And this one, standing outside the gate of that gastly-looking house—"

"Auntie Louie's," Charley murmured.

"Is it? Oh, sorry! But it does look rather ghastly, sort of grim and don't-you-dare-come-in. Does it really look like that? No, it can't if it's in Bell Lane—"

"It did when I saw it," Charley said emphatically.

"Of course, sorry! I'm an awful oaf. I like this one, too, the girl with flowers in her hair, running through the wood with the fawn. And the one where she's lying asleep under a tree with orange berries, with the fawn sitting beside her." He turned the pages back. "Oh, and this one near the beginning! The fawn looking over the gate at all those funny little people in the garden. That reminds me of a queer old boy who lives up beyond Bartlett's. He's got a garden full of horrific little gnomes, all painted in hideous bright colors. Nobody knows where he got them all from because he's a hermit and never speaks to anyone, but I believe the village kids tease him about them a lot."

"It's a rotten shame if they do!" said Charley, suddenly hotly angry. "He made them all himself. He told me so!"

John looked at her in astonishment. "Do you mean he *talked* to you? Well I'm blowed! What did he say?"

"I'll tell you when I remember," said Charley. "It was good. I learned it by heart, but I've forgotten it for the minute."

He laughed, not taking her seriously, and turned to the book again. "This is a super idea, you know. A sort of fairy story and picture diary combined. I like it a lot. So will Miss Whatsername. Well—there's your holiday task."

"I hate that word," she said.

"So do I. Take no notice of it."

"And I didn't do it for her."

"Does that matter?"

"Yes. It doesn't seem fair. I ought to have done something specially—if I was going to, but I wasn't."

"Who did you do this for?"

She stared at him. "Nobody. Just me."

"Why? Why did you do it?"

She thought of all the reasons. Because she could put into a picture things she could never put into words. Because sometimes, afterward, it had helped to paint the very things that had frightened her. Because she had been able to paint what she liked without people asking silly questions. She hesitated, wondering whether to give him the last reason, then said, defensively, "Because I wanted to."

"Exactly!" He laughed. "And what better reason could you possibly have for doing some jolly nice painting? Look here"—he was deadly serious now—"I don't suppose anyone who ever did anything worth doing—painting, music, writing, anything like that— ever did it for anyone else. It's just lucky if other people like it when you've done it, that's all." He handed it back to her. "I think a lot of people will like this. What are you going to call it?"

She looked at him doubtfully; then her eyes widened suddenly. He nodded, smiling, as if he knew the thought that had just come into her mind. "*Could* I?"

He laughed. "Why not? I don't think it's quite the

same kind of fawn as Debussy was thinking about, but that doesn't matter. This is your fawn. It's your own. And it's your book."

"But the music? The music seemed right for mine . . ."

"Of course." He took out his pen and handed it to her. "Here, write it down while you remember it. You've heard it often enough, now see if you can spell it!"

Charley took the pen and wrote carefully across the front page of her book *"L'Après-Midi d'un Faune."* She thought for a moment, chuckled, then added *"by Rowan Weston."* "I'm called Charley at school usually," she said. "They'll think it's a new girl!"

30

Home with Aunt Emm

John had gone—looking like someone quite different, in a gray suit, with a mackintosh over his arm and carrying a briefcase. Charley had felt almost awed at the sight of him.

At the last minute she had dashed after him. "John, wait! I've just remembered—what the old man said!" She had paused, drawn a deep breath, then gabbled, "It-ain't-what-you've-got-nor-where-you-go-what-counts. It's-what-you-do-with-what-you've-got, wherever-you-happens-to-be!"

"I say, that's splendid! Say it again—no, there isn't time. Write it to me, will you?"

"Yes! Will you write back?"

"Would you like me to?"

"*Please.*"

Her eyes had misted over then, so that she had seen only a gray blur as he got into the car. She had picked up Bogey, rubbing her cheek against his coat and holding his paw to make him wave, and by the time the mist had cleared, John had gone.

And now Charley was going, too. Aunt Emm had come down in time for lunch, Mrs. Denning had driven them to the station to catch the afternoon train, had seen them into the corner seats of an empty compartment, and stayed to see them off.

"So now everything's all right, isn't it?" she had said with unexpected gentleness, as she kissed Charley good-bye. "And you must come again—for a proper visit next time!" The train had moved off; Charley had waved until Mrs. Denning was out of sight, then sat down in her corner seat.

So now everything was all right. Mrs. Denning had asked her to come again, John had said he would write to her, and Auntie Louie had wanted her after all . . .

Charley stared out the window at the passing fields and winding lanes. Late-autumn sunshine flicked down through the trees that lined the embankment, and on the patches of bracken between. It was fawns' country, it was a fawn's afternoon . . . *L'après-midi d'un faune.*

It was tempting to think that everything was all right now—like a happy ending to a story. But it was not all right. Auntie Louie had wanted her, but Aunt Emm had not. And she was going home with Aunt Emm, who still didn't want her. She didn't want Aunt Emm either, but that was different. Nobody did. Even Mrs. Scrotton didn't like her. But it was all right for Aunt Emm. She was grown-up—quite old. She must be used to it by now.

Aunt Emm tapped her on the knee and Charley saw that she was offering her a mint humbug. She took one, unwrapped it, and put it in her mouth. The warm, chewy satisfaction of it comforted her. Well, so what? she thought. Nobody could be wanted by everybody, all the time. But not to be wanted by *anybody.* . . .

She glanced across at Aunt Emm. She, too, was sucking a mint humbug, her cheek swelled out at one side, her eyes staring vacantly at the telegraph wires flashing past the window. She looked as if she, too, might be finding some satisfaction, some comfort, in the warm chewing. Charley stared. Somehow, sucking a sweet like that, Aunt Emm looked different— hardly old at all. She looked the way Charley was feeling—as if she was hating going back with someone who didn't like her, to a place where she wasn't wanted . . .

Charley suddenly remembered something. She got up and opened her case. Then she laid a small, flat parcel in Aunt Emm's lap.

"That's for you," she said. "I got it in Frickham."

"For me?" Aunt Emm looked quite startled. "But what is it?"

"I—I think it's a sort of lavender bag thing. You know, to smell nice. You can hang it up."

Aunt Emm's face went a patchy red and her mouth twitched slightly. She lifted the lavender bag to her nose and sniffed at it. "It does! It smells very nice. It must have cost you quite a lot."

"It's all right. I just thought it was quite pretty—"

"It is. It is. Very— I could put it with my handkerchiefs."

"Yes. Or hang it up."

Aunt Emm fingered the lace edging and bent over it, looking at it closely. "How nice. How very nice. And real satin ribbon! How cleverly they make these things nowadays—by machine, I suppose. And these tiny flowers in the lace . . ." She seemed not to want to look up again just yet. Charley leaned forward too.

"Yes, I think they're meant to be forget-me-nots—"

"Or rosebuds, perhaps? They're pink—"

"Oh, yes—of course."

Together they examined it minutely. Then, carefully, Aunt Emm wrapped it up again in its tissue paper, and folded her hands over it in her lap. She looked up at last, and gave Charley a sudden, twisted little smile.

"Thank you," she said.

"It's all right," said Charley.

Aunt Emm closed her eyes, and Charley leaned back with a sigh of relief.

It was all right.

THE AUTHOR

JOAN G. ROBINSON is the author of *When Marnie Was There*, the story of a young girl and her imagination, and the *Mary, Mary Stories*, a book for younger readers. She lives in Norfolk, England, in a house called the Unicorn House.

THE ARTIST

PRUDENCE SEWARD, a member of the Royal Watercolor Society and the Society of Painter-Etchers and Engravers, was educated at Northwood College, Harrow Art School and the Royal College of Art. Her fine line drawings add greatly to the charm of this book.

THORNLEY

Old Man's cottage

Mrs Denning's

The Horseshoe.

Bartlett's

Summerhouse

Scarecrow

A Map of the
neighbourhood
where Charley
spent her
unusual holiday

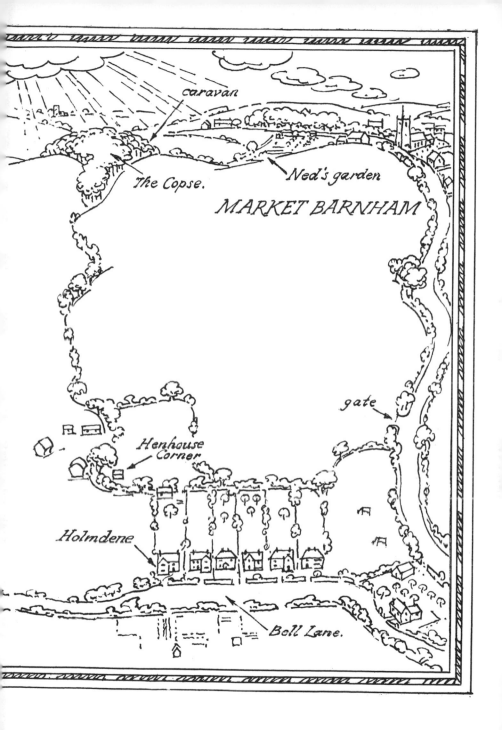

caravan

The Copse.

Ned's garden

MARKET BARNHAM

gate

Henhouse Corner

Holmdene

Boll Lane.